Turn Northward, Love

Turn Northward, Love

RUTH GLOVER

Beacon Hill Press of Kansas City
Kansas City, Missouri

Copyright 1996
by Beacon Hill Press of Kansas City

ISBN 083-411-5905

Printed in the
United States of America

Cover design: Mike Walsh
Cover illustration: Keith Alexander

Library of Congress Cataloging-in-Publication Data
Glover, Ruth.
    Turn northward, love / Ruth Glover.
        p.   cm. — (The wildrose series ; bk. 4)
    ISBN 0-8341-1590-5
    I. Title.   II. Series: Glover, Ruth. Wildrose series ; bk. 4.
    PS3557.L678T87   1996
    813'.54—dc21   96-39247
                                                                 CIP

10   9   8   7   6   5   4   3   2   1

And they shall be mine, saith the LORD *of hosts,*
in that day when I make up my jewels.
—Mal. 3:17

For my grandchildren, His jewels—
Ben, Kristen, Shannon, Jeremy, Jeff, Ashley,
and Ryan

ABOUT THE AUTHOR

Ruth Glover's recollections of the Saskatchewan bush country of the 1920s and 1930s include details of the region's isolation. The lack of doctors was a particular hardship especially in the winter, when snow and extreme cold made travel to the nearest doctor, 20 miles away in Prince Albert, possible only by a horse-drawn sleigh or cutter. Residents often had to get by without professional medical help—or at least deal with the situation as best they could—until they could make the journey to Prince Albert.

"I remember a hired man who somehow got his ankles tangled up in a reaper," Mrs. Glover comments. "He managed to crawl across the field to get help. Fortunately, he escaped a dangerous bull that was pastured in that field—that's one thing we kids always remembered about that incident. He then had to be taken clear to Prince Albert for medical treatment."

Similar physical dangers, far from the convenient reach of doctors, sometimes visited Mrs. Glover's family, the Vogts. The family was often forced to make do with their own medical treatments and relied heavily on prayer. "My brother Al, whom we called 'Junior,' once suffered a jagged tear in his lower arm that occurred in the chicken coop. It was only my mother's prayers that got him through. And once my brother Fred cut off the tip of one of his fingers while sawing wood. I remember him soaking it, and it healed nicely in time."

A particular curiosity of the bush was "the great plethora of men," according to Mrs. Glover. "It was pretty well balanced out by the time I was growing up, but in the earlier years a lot of single men came to settle the area. They didn't last long without women—they had to make a 'home.' So the supplies of available single young women were snatched up quickly. It was not uncommon then for marriages to be arranged, often by the young man and young woman writing to each other first, and some proposals actually being made by correspondence. It is also interesting to note that many books mention that numerous prairie homes had a former teacher as a wife and mother—because they were married off quickly after coming to a community to teach."

The lack of nearby doctors and the overbalance of men to women figure significantly in this fourth of Ruth Glover's Wildrose Series novels.

Mrs. Glover lives in The Dalles, Oregon, with her pastor husband, Hal. She is a contributor to numerous Christian publications. The couple have three children and seven grandchildren.

1

AS HER AGILE FINGERS MOVED OVER THE STORE shelves and counters, Hannah Vaughn cast a quick glance at the clock above the heavy brass cash register. Ten minutes until opening time. Even now she could see a few impatient customers through the fancy etched glass of the double doors, awaiting the striking of the clock—marking another day of business for Vaughn's Royal Emporium.

Ten minutes, and time for a few more of the memories that seemed to crowd the aisles and hover in the air today. Hannah didn't know why, on this particular day, the past pressed in so insistently. Perhaps it was the letter crackling at times in her skirt pocket.

And the clock—elegant, of course, and fitting for such a refined enterprise, its tick heard readily above the subdued voices of the busy clerks—had struck off minute by minute, hour by hour, day by day, and month by month the inexorable march of time since she had entered these doors as worker and eventually as owner.

Nothing was too fine for Morris Vaughn and the dreams he had cherished when, as a young man with a small inheritance, he had come west to the growing town of Mayfair, recognized its possibilities, and settled down. Here, in line with his plans and purposes, he had met and married the town's prettiest girl. Here he had built his empire. And here he was buried.

Here his one disappointment, his only child, had been consigned to spend her hours, her weeks, her months, and her years. Here his Perpetual Calendar Clock, in its elegantly carved solid oak case and "guaranteed to be thoroughly reliable and accurate," had hypnotically and relentlessly counted away Hannah's life from midteens to mid-20s.

Hannah wasn't aware that she avoided looking at herself in the tall mirror that was placed strategically behind the display of "Wonderful Bargains in Ladies' Neckwear." She worked automatically, straightening the "Novelties that will be worn by everyone this year."

Everyone but me, she thought briefly, adjusting the white collar of her serviceable gray dress but doing it without benefit of the looking glass.

She couldn't help smiling a bit as she pictured herself in the "Nobby new swell collarette." Its square yoke, she was sure, would only emphasize the squareness of her jaw. Its alternate rows of satin and butter-colored insertions in some respects matched her pale face. And the wide, flaring, six-inch ruffle of open oriental lace could only draw attention to her shoulders, already too broad to conform to the admired female figure with its graceful neck slanting to rounded shoulders, full bosom, small waist, swelling hips, and, finally, dainty feet.

Hannah's feet, today as every day, were laced in their Goodyear brand "very durable shoes for general wear," and several additional pairs, no more feminine, awaited their turn in her closet in Vaughn House.

Her waist, narrow enough, was scarcely wider than the parts of her above and below it. "Slim," her friends Pansy and Gussie always maintained stoutly; "Skin and bones," her father had said. And having said it fixed it indelibly in Hannah's mind.

That her shoulders were straight was not because of any instinct on her part to hold herself proudly erect.

Rather, it was the result of years of enduring the stricture of the "Gamble Shoulder Brace."

Growing tall, Hannah had drooped in an unconscious attempt to be like her pretty, petite mother, so adored by her husband. Longing to be like the mother, Hannah resembled the father, a father who wished fervently (and audibly) that the daughter were more like the mother.

As Hannah grew tall, thin, and "ordinary" (her father's word), the likeness to the father and the dissimilarity to the mother was pronounced. The father's high complexion, however, faded to pallor in his daughter. A "creamy pallor," Pansy and Gussie insisted, but a pallor nevertheless. What was a magnificent nose on the man was a very ordinary feature on the face of the girl. His square jaw was muted to gentler proportions, his blazing blue eyes were muted to a blue-gray, and his chin, so firm and arrogant, on his daughter was simply an ordinary chin.

And "ordinary" was Morris Vaughn's frank assessment of the child who, in spite of everything, adored him. Following her father around, dumbly seeking a crumb of approval, running his errands happily if it meant a careless pat on the shoulder, the child starved on a skimpy diet of the love and attention she craved. "Ordinary" to Morris Vaughn was a dirty word.

Mirrors, it seemed, had been part of several pivotal moments in Hannah's life. Perhaps they had been to blame. Perhaps her father, viewing himself with complete satisfaction and noting the small child or the growing girl in his shadow—so clearly humble, so plainly *plain*—had felt prompted to the responses that had stung then and just as surely stung now.

"There's nothing that adds *presence* to a room like a handsome mirror," Morris Vaughn had said the day he hung the heavily gilded, rococo mirror over the mantel in the parlor of Vaughn House. Stepping back, he had admired not only himself in its reflection but also the richly

furnished room behind him. His gaze shifted to the dim
outline of his hovering wife and his daughter. A pained expression darkened his face.

"Amy," he had said harshly, "can't you do something
about this?"

"This?" queried the timid Amy.

"This!" Morris's disapproving look and the finger pointing in her direction sent Hannah's already bent shoulders further floorward; her "mop" (her father's oft-used word) of hair
fell forward, hiding the quick rush of color to her pale face.

"Straighten your shoulders, Hannah, for heaven's
sake!" the man continued. "When you slouch like that, it
only serves to emphasize your height! And your bosom
simply disappears—"

Hannah's flushed face paled. To a developing child,
not at ease with her changing body and bound in her
thinking by the Victorian regulations of the day, her father's remark—instantly and forever—made horrid and
obscene what had been meant to be beautiful.

"Morris—," fluttered the blushing Amy in a feeble attempt to stem the tirade.

"Hush, my dear. I have her good at heart. Surely you
know that!"

And the disapproval in Morris's eyes turned on his
wife.

"Of course, my dear, of course," and Amy back-ped-
aled quickly.

"My deep desire is that she be beautiful," Morris said,
graciously accepting his wife's submission to his better
judgment. "Now, as to these—" He indicated the hair ribbon that Hannah had so carefully fastened in her "mop"
that morning and the ruffles she had cherished on the dainty pink pinafore. "These have got to go. Never have I seen
anything less fitting!" Morris made a grimace of distaste.

"Surely you can see," he continued firmly, "that we
have here a . . ."

Even Morris wasn't cruel enough to say "ugly."

"Here we have a—a duckling, not a swan. Just remove these folderols, my dear, and eliminate the gewgaws."

Hannah's heart broke; her one claim to beauty, she felt, were the dainty accouterments of femininity she could put on with her clothes every morning; these people would see and comment on. "How pretty!" they would say. Hannah hid behind the frilly facade; it was her shield. Without these attractive appendages, she was just plain Hannah, obviously not enough in itself to be accepted.

"As for her posture," Morris tutted, "we can—we must—do something about that."

He studied the forlorn figure standing before him on his extravagant Brussels carpet, surrounded by the rare treasures and rich trappings he had acquired (including Amy), and was frustrated that he couldn't at will produce a fitting offspring. With all his power and authority, it was the one area in which he was helpless. But he would do his best!

"I'll order the Gamble Back Brace," he decided thoughtfully.

And Morris Vaughn, who never "let the grass grow under his feet," who was "a man of action," and with whom "no sooner said than done" was a shibboleth, once again put action to words.

The brace, promptly ordered through the store and donned by the shrinking Hannah with her mother's sighing assistance, was advertised to be "the most comfortable and effective brace ever made. Its two finely tempered steel springs," it claimed, "would act the same as if you gently press your thumbs on one's shoulder blades, throwing the chest out and the shoulders back."

In reality, it had been torture, not only to the thin shoulders but also to the equally poorly developed emotions of a child who would rather shrink than flaunt, but who must now emphasize a particularly sensitive area of her anatomy.

Pansy and Gussie, ever her faithful friends, had wept with Hannah in her pain and shuddered with her in her humiliation.

"I suppose," Gussie said fiercely, "he'd bind your feet, like in China, if the store carried bindings!"

"You mustn't say things like that," Hannah had pleaded, tucking her generous feet under her. "He just wants me . . . you see . . . to be beautiful."

"You're *already* beautiful," insisted loyal Pansy.

But Hannah had shaken her head. "Not yet . . . ," she said, and endured the brace.

Now—her shoulders undeniably straight—Hannah moved from the tidy neckwear department to the millinery department. And "not yet," she thought as her eyes, in spite of herself, flickered momentarily to the mirror above the "new and very swell hats" on display.

Nobby must be in style, she thought, briefly diverted from her reminiscences as she put into place a hat thus termed. Made of straw, with a pleating of silk net around the crown, coils of ribbon and net around the edge, turned up in back, and finished with a bunch of violets and a large rosette of lace, the "Nobby" fashion competed with The Louette, The Evette, The Swell Evangeline, and others, for the attention of Mayfair's most fastidious clientele.

Imagining the reaction of the Reverend Delbert Bly if she should turn up in church in the "Nobby," Hannah gave a small, involuntary laugh, causing a nearby clerk to smile at her cheerily. *If* Delbert should ever get around to proposing, and *if* she accepted him, she would have no trouble fitting the mold of a parson's wife. Delbert's expectations were not a great deal different than Papa's had been. And again Hannah's hand went to her virginal collar, crisp and white but unadorned by the smallest edging. Delbert looked on her with approval, if not with love. Was it enough? Had it been enough with Papa? Hannah's empty heart held the answer her lips had never been able to express.

Delbert, of course, was much kinder than Papa had ever been. Was kindness enough?

At least with Delbert it wasn't her money. Or was it? Hannah put the suggestion out of her mind with a feeling of shame.

But the church needed so many things—a new roof, yearly tuning for the piano. And Delbert's dream—an organ for the sanctuary! Hannah's money could do so much. But its availability obviously wasn't compelling where Delbert was concerned. Four years, and he was still cautious when it came to pinpointing his intentions. He was so cautious, in fact, and so deliberate in his whole approach to remarriage, that Hannah at times felt she would scream.

Not that she was at all sure she would accept a proposal from the minister. But to be kept dangling—it was, she felt, humiliating.

Where was approval? Where was enthusiasm? Where was—where was passion? In short, where was love?

But what Delbert would offer—kindness, companionship, the opportunity to be part of a family again, to have children—had an appeal to one without them.

At least Delbert was honest. And that, she admitted bitterly, had not been the case with her other suitors—suitors who had made their appearance startlingly soon after the death of her father and the newspaper's announcement of her inheritance of all he had amassed, including Vaughn's Royal Emporium.

The middle-aged proprietor of a competing dry good store, a store that was far less classy than Vaughn's and reported to be in financial difficulties, had not been slow in coming forward with his plan. Crudely, it amounted to an alliance—in marriage and in business.

The second swain had been far more crafty. And far more hurtful.

Young, handsome, well-dressed, Burt Nesselrode stepped smoothly and gallantly into Hannah's lonely life.

As he wined and dined her, feted and courted her, his attentions had found a budding response in Hannah's bleak heart. Only when reports reached her from numerous sources that the man was a gambler and a charlatan, owing countless debts in town and under great pressure to pay up, did Hannah make the connection between the attractiveness of her money and her own lack of personal attractions. Having begun feeling like a queen, Hannah sank to feeling like a peasant—poor.

Yes, Delbert was honest; about that she need have no questions. Bloodless, perhaps, and maddeningly dispassionate, but honest.

"The man's a vegetable!" Pansy was wont to say. "A . . . a potato!"

And Hannah always laughed. But it was a rueful laugh. Behind it was, again, a recognition of the old familiar sensation of being humiliated. How long should a girl—a woman—linger around, waiting for a declaration of a man's intentions? And did she even want Delbert Bly's attentions, and would they, if offered, satisfy the need in her hungry heart?

Pansy, now a married woman with two small children, was sure they would not. "It's not enough, Hannah," she insisted. "Everyone deserves a real love affair. *You* deserve it."

And Pansy's eyes grew soft with the warmth of her own continuing love affair with Buell. Hannah had lived through that love affair and warmed her heart at its fire and knew she didn't want to settle for less.

Gussie, too, had fallen in love—fallen so completely that she had fully and freely separated herself from her family and friends, leaving with her new husband for a life of some deprivation, much hard work, and deep satisfaction in a small community in the vast Northwest Territories. A community all but hidden in the heart of the bush. A community called Wildrose.

THE SMELL OF ALL OUTDOORS—SWEET WITH NEW lilacs bursting into bloom at the corner of the house—drew Gussie to the door. With hands soapy from the breakfast dishwater, she thrust open the screen and stepped out onto the covered entranceway to the sturdy log house at her back, wiping her hands on her skirt.

In spite of her loneliness at times, Gussie never regretted exchanging the unending vistas of the prairie for the seclusion of the bush. That the seclusion was oppressive, even intimidating, to some people, she understood. But having come as a bride, motivated by love and loyalty and willing to make any sacrifice, Gussie had been surprised, then delighted, to find herself surrendering to the beauty of the bush.

Added to that was her contentment. Henry, her husband, was so clearly realizing the fulfillment of his dreams, and she so wholeheartedly shared them, that nothing else was more enticing than her small bush-encircled domain.

And small Henry—Hanky, she fondly called him—had made his appearance to complete her happiness and tie her even more closely to Wildrose. This small farm, so painfully grub-hoed of its bushes, its poplars and birches slowly giving way to fields and pastures, would be Hanky's inheritance. Hanky and his sibling—and Gussie's hard, small hand pressed the bulge below her apron, and her heart, already full to overflowing, enlarged to include one more. At *least* one more, she thought, mentally counting small unborn Chapmans.

Filled with her own pleasure over the coming baby, Gussie's thoughts turned very naturally to her neighbor. Lifting her gaze eastward, Gussie could see the thin stream of smoke from the Ivey chimney. Planning a clearing for the placement of their house, Henry had chosen an area abutting the Ivey property. Almost always that smoke warmed Gussie's heart. At times she could hear a faint sound of machinery or a lifted voice. The sounds righted her tipping world when it seemed lonesomely out of balance. Visits back and forth were cherished as highlights not only for her, but, she knew, for Dovie. Dovie had no baby voice to fill her vacuum of silence with welcome demands.

"It'll be good to have close neighbors," Henry had said, stepping off the area of the foundation. And Digby Ivey had been quick to offer help. Having been one of the first settlers to the area, his advice was wise, and his encouragement, especially through the first hard year, had helped his young neighbors hold steady.

Of course, farms here in the bush country were small in comparison to the spreading acres coming under cultivation on the prairies to the south. But to the land-hungry and often penniless immigrant, such a farm was within reach and manageable.

The basic unit under the land policy of the dominion was the township. Six miles square, it was divided into 36 sections of 640 acres each. A free grant under the homestead system provided that a settler could obtain 160 acres for a payment of a $10 patent fee, three years' residence, and cultivation.

In spite of this—although a floodtide of settlements was taking place in the remaining unoccupied lands of the United States—only a trickle flowed into the beckoning Northwest Territories. This was in part because of the unfavorable publicity concerning "country about as forbidding as any on earth" reported by some disgruntled or overwhelmed pioneer. "In Manitoba," it was proclaimed in an English journal, "those who are not frozen to death are often maimed for life by frostbites."

Gussie was neither frozen or maimed. Her small Saskatchewan home was snug and warm in winter. As long, that is, as the fires were blazing and the doors closed. Even now Henry was engaged in the never-ending chore of felling trees, necessary not only for fuel but also to fulfill his pledge to clear his land and plant his crops.

But accidents happened, and tragedy struck from time to time, and nothing could be worse than to be isolated and alone, without help. And if not help, sympathy. So Gussie was not only pleased but also relieved to know that just beyond a thick stand of poplars, Ivey land began.

It seemed, however, that rather than Gussie and Henry needing help, it was their neighbors who had suffered through difficult times. Henry and Gussie reached out to Digby and Dovie.

Sensing a small flutter beneath her apron, Gussie's thoughts turned with concern to Dovie Ivey. Was Dovie standing on *her* porch, she wondered, likewise pressing a hand to her expected baby? If so, it would be with considerable, but well-concealed, concern. Although Dovie maintained a brave front, Gussie knew the underlying worry, even desperation, that Dovie harbored. This pregnancy, after all, was Dovie's third, and according to Dovie's painfully imparted confidence, her final chance at a child of her own.

"Digby insists this is it," Dovie had half-whispered, her eyes tragic as she faced the unacceptable possibility of never having a child of her own. Digby's son, almost a man and helping with the cultivation and development of Dovie's sisters' farm, had never been cuddled in Dovie's hungry arms. Dovie, past 40, had married Digby three years ago. Three years of marriage and three pregnancies. Dovie felt an urgency about the matter, and rightly so.

"Time is running out, Gussie!" Dovie had cried.

But how many more times would Digby stand by an open grave and share his wife's anguish? "This is the last time," he kindly but firmly maintained.

Gussie turned to her kitchen and the small boy making mush of his oatmeal. With more patience than usual, she washed sticky blobs from his soft hair, pink face, and fat hands and set him down with an unusually long hug. His very resistance spoke of his health and normalcy. Finally she released him to balance on unsteady feet and lunge off in pursuit of a wise and fleeing cat.

At midmorning Gussie put Hanky and a lunch pail in a sturdy red wagon and pulled the gabbling child through the bush that circled their home, toward the distant sound of Henry's ax.

Seated under a tree at the edge of the clearing, keeping a wary eye on the playing child and dog and handing her husband the biscuits she had buttered and jammed and the bottle of milk she had taken at the last minute from the well's cold depths, Gussie talked about her concern for her friend.

"It's not long now for Dovie," she said. "Just six weeks or so. Oh, Henry—I pray everything goes well this time! I think it will just kill Dovie if she loses another baby!"

Henry, his mouth full, nodded.

"It would be different, Henry, if she were my age. Not that anyone can accept the loss of a child at any age. But at least there would be hope of another eventually. She hasn't even had time to properly heal between babies—she's been in such a fret that time will run out on her. You know, Henry, she considers each pregnancy a miracle. It isn't likely she'll have another chance."

"Digby says not, of course," Henry reminded her, "regardless of her age."

Not that Digby had said that to *him*, but Henry knew the conversations Gussie and Dovie shared. With very little other company, especially in the long winter months, Henry treasured the open communication he shared with his wife. What a joy—or a horror—intimacy could be! Henry laid his hand, battered and calloused, on his wife's swelling stomach in confirmation of that sweet intimacy.

"I'm just disgustingly healthy," Gussie said contentedly.

"Thank God," was Henry's response.

Yes, thank God. Infant mortality in the Territories, as in all places where medical science and doctors were unavailable, was high. Many a home carried on as best it could when a mother died in childbed.

The lack of medical help was of the gravest concern not only to settlers but to officials in the Northwest. In 1885 the Medical Practitioners' Ordinance made mandatory the registration of doctors in order that they might practice legally. But even in 1894, only 36 doctors gave their addresses as being in the Saskatchewan area. Dovie's baby, as Gussie's, would be delivered by Dovie's sister Anna, the nearest to a nurse or doctor the community boasted.

And in Gussie's case it was enough. Dovie, however, had delivered two babies too early; neither had drawn breath. Dovie's grief had been terrible to witness. Her spinster sisters, Anna, and Dovie's twin, Dulcie, had been equally heartbroken. But they had rallied to be the stabilizing support their sister needed. Gussie, too, offered warm arms, earnest prayers, and encouraging words. But often she felt guilty—guilty. Guilty because her arms were filled with the charm and sweetness of small Henry while Dovie's arms were empty. But Dovie loved "Hanky" and encouraged Gussie's visits.

After each sorrow, Dovie's slender thread of hope had been "Next time . . ."

Now even that consolation was gone; Digby, in his 50s

and deeply in love with his bouncy, usually cheerful little wife, was terribly afraid he would lose her. "The last time," he had said, and watched over Dovie with tender concern.

✳ ✳ ✳

Gussie was kneeling in the garden when she heard the clip-clop of a horse's hooves. About to pinch off a decent-sized lettuce leaf from the early planting, just now showing signs of maturing and mouth-watering in its appeal to appetites long starved for anything green, she paused and glanced up. The beautiful bay could belong only to Matthew Hunter. Along with the farming necessary to "prove" up his land, Matthew also bred thoroughbred horses. This one, stepping high, was no handsomer than the rider who sat the saddle with grace and reined in the impatient steed with a strong hand.

"Mornin', ma'am," he said, doffing his hat so that his black, curly hair gleamed in the noon sun.

"Good morning, *sir*," Gussie said with a laugh as she got to her feet, the succulent greens between her fingers.

Matthew Hunter's hearty laugh followed. "Well, Gussie," he said, "looks like you're getting ready to put together a remarkable dinner."

"You wouldn't be willing to eat with us, now would you, Matthew?"

"No need to beg, Gussie."

"Get down, Matthew, and come on in. Henry will be in from the clearing any time."

"Where's the young'un?"

"Down for his nap. You've heard of making hay while the sun shines? I make dinner while the son sleeps."

Matthew shook his head over the attempted witticism. "I hope you cook better than you joke," he offered.

"You know I do, Matthew. Come on now—get down."

"I'll go and meet Henry—have a little business to talk over with him."

"Monkey business, I'll be bound," Gussie murmured, but low enough so that this second, sillier joke went unheard. She knew it would be horse business. Henry was eager to upgrade his rather sorry team.

Matthew, his white teeth flashing in his dark face, loosed the reins, and his magnificent mount bounded ahead toward the clearing where Henry, between usual farm tasks, was clearing additional land.

Being more than 21, a male, and having paid the required $10 fee, Henry, as well as others like him, were guaranteed by the Land Act a free title for his quarter section of good, black, Saskatchewan soil if at the end of three years he had cultivated part of his land and done some building. It was not easy work; many a homestead sat partly cleared with bush regaining ground quickly when a settler, often a city man and unused to hardship and deprivation, had buckled under and quit.

But others were moving in. At first, in spite of the attractive offer, only a few settlers had come. They had worked their land with the precious Prairie Queen plough and oxen, because oxen needed no oats but could live off the land. The first tents had been replaced with soddies on the prairie and dugouts in the bush, and eventually, in the bush, by log houses. Now the narrow angle of land between the North and the South Branches of the Saskatchewan River—commonly referred to as "the bush" and more euphemistically known as the "parkland"—was filling rapidly.

It was a hard life, making men and women of character or breaking them. Drought, ill health, or their own ineptitude caused many to seek an easier way. Those who remained had to deal with hordes of mosquitoes, gophers and mice, a short growing season, and a long winter. Henry was one of the survivors.

And so was Matthew Hunter. He had in fact survived longer than Henry and could be called "established." Now his horse-breeding venture was beginning to pay off for him and for those fortunate enough to obtain one of his thoroughbreds. All he lacked, he thought now bitterly, was a wife.

At one time, before the accident, that had been the least of his worries. Every girl he met, it seemed, flashed her dimples at him, gave him "come-hither" looks, and let him know in undeniable ways that she was available. There was a time, he thought again, that he could have had his pick of any girl in the Territories.

Where were they now? Was a man to be judged entirely on a handsome, unmarred face—a masculine, athletic physique? Was love, after all, the beautiful thing poets wrote about, musicians memorialized in song, and novels described in such glowing terms?

Thank God, Matthew thought, he had found out in time. Thank God he had been saved from a union with one of those empty-headed females who had withdrawn so quickly after the accident eight years ago. And yet he was the same man—a better man, he dared think. A better, wiser man. A lonely man . . .

Gussie quickly added another plate to the table, rinsed the lettuce, and added vinegar and oil—a dish fit for a king!—and, frowning at the pan of potatoes and onions left over from last year's crop, she visited the well. Drawing up the pail that kept her perishables cold, Gussie withdrew the small remaining portion of a venison roast, cut off a piece, replaced the meat, lowered the pail to its shelf, and hurried back to the house. Along with a quickly opened jar of tomatoes, the meat was added to the potato mixture to make, she felt, a creditable slumgullion.

This, with home-baked bread and a small dish each of wild strawberries that she had been planning for their evening meal but would gladly share now, would be the best she had to offer—and much better, she knew, than the bachelor fare Matthew usually ate.

The coffee was boiling when the men trooped in,

washed at the basin of warm water Gussie provided, and turned with appreciative sniffs to the round oak table. After Henry asked a blessing on the food, it was "Make yourself at home!" which Matthew proceeded to do, having been a guest on many occasions.

When halfway through the meal small Henry awoke and was brought to the table, he smiled a sleepy grin upon seeing Matthew and held out his arms.

As Matthew cuddled the child, eating "piecemeal" and offering tidbits to Hanky, Gussie studied him, oblivious to the farm talk of the two men.

A wonderful man, she thought, *and a handsome one, in spite of the accident. Before it, he must have been an Adonis.*

From all accounts he had been, in earlier days, the most sought-after young man around. Gussie's loyal heart hardened when she recalled the explanation Matthew had made, lightheartedly, about his present "expectations."

"Can't blame the ladies," he had said. "Wouldn't be too pleasant to wake up and see this face on the pillow beside you."

"Bosh!" Gussie had cried, in much the same way she had defended her girlhood friend Hannah across the years.

Now, thinking of Hannah, Gussie recognized the beginning of an idea—an idea that could benefit both of her friends.

"Matthew," she said thoughtfully, "see how Hanky loves you. You really should be a father."

"I suppose so," Matthew agreed. "After all, the Bible urges being fruitful and multiplying."

"You haven't been doing your share, my friend," Henry offered with a grin.

"And probably won't," Matthew said, again lightly, as he usually did when marriage and women were mentioned.

"But why, Matthew?" Gussie asked vigorously. "There are girls—women—available. Why, there's Nora Kreb—

pretty enough and looking—yes, looking—for a husband. There's Dilly Bradford—"

"Gussie," Matthew said slowly, "let me say it straight out—I dated both those women. I say 'dated'—I mean 'kept company with'—both of them. And plenty of others. I guess as a youth I was tremendously self-confident—not conceited, but taking good looks for granted. *And* the interest, even the adoration, of girls by the score." Matthew smiled crookedly.

"Oh, Matthew," Gussie, so used to commiserating with her friend Hannah, said. "You're too hard on yourself, I'm sure."

"Not really," Matthew said objectively. "I was quite the cock-of-the-walk in those days. Well," his voice hardened, "it took the accident to let the plain truth sink in: None of them seemed willing to love me for what I was, *inside*. Maybe what I was inside wasn't all that great. I've been working on that. *God's* been working on that. I'm a better man for what happened. But, to date, it hasn't won me any laurels with the gentler sex."

"You don't give them a chance, Matthew!"

"Perhaps. Once burned, twice shy, I guess. Now, Gussie, if there were any more like you—"

"There are!" Gussie interrupted with enthusiasm.

Matthew quirked an amused eyebrow at her.

"It's Hannah, Henry. Hannah would be perfect! That's my friend, back in Manitoba, Matthew. Hannah is a jewel!"

"And single?" Matthew asked dryly.

"But that's because she *is* such a jewel!" Gussie explained. "Matthew, believe me—Hannah would be just right for you!"

Matthew looked at Henry, who was nodding agreement, and shrugged.

"But she's in Manitoba and I'm in Saskatchewan. Too far away to—well, to check out," Matthew finished somewhat lamely.

"But you can write! Oh, Matthew, say you will! Let me write Hannah and see if she's willing to correspond with you!"

Matthew was silent. Finally, slowly, he said, "No harm in writing, I suppose. But, Gussie," he added with voice firmed, "you mustn't tell her about the accident. When and if I marry, it will be to a lady who loves me for what I am, not for what I may or may not look like. Understood?"

"Understood!" And Gussie, aglow with success and eager to put pen to paper, began clearing the table.

Matthew set Hanky on his feet, thanked Gussie for the meal, and added, "Please, my friends—pray with me about this."

And Gussie and Henry, knowing their friend's earnest commitment to Christ and the growth he had made over the last three years of their relationship, readily agreed. Matthew indeed was more concerned with the beauty of the inner person than the external, fading, deceptive outward appearance.

"Perfect! Just perfect for Hannah!" Gussie breathed.

Gussie flew through another round of dishwashing and wiping, rinsed a pan of beans that had been soaking and put them to boil, pulled out the button box that was held in reserve for times when special concentration was needed, and set Hanky to sorting them into fascinating heaps.

Then, with a feeling of destiny, she sat down at the table to write her dear, distant friend.

"Dear Hannah: Now hear me out before you throw this away . . ."

* * *

With Gussie's good food inside him and the well-wishes of his friends ringing in his ears, Matthew turned his mount toward home. As usual, it took awhile to bring the fractious horse under control, and he gave himself to the pleasure of an experience as different from a plow horse's performance as a butterfly's dance is from a caterpillar's crawl. His initial investment was paying off; his blooded horses were sought eagerly for riding and breeding purposes. Moreover, there was his own intense satisfaction in the beautiful creatures. A lonely man in most ways, Matthew's thoroughbreds absorbed some of the passion that was within him.

Now the horse between his firm knees lifted dainty hooves, arched its neck against the rein, and settled for a mincing walk. Only then did Matthew's hold relax; only then did he think back to the first high-strung horse, his own ineptness, and the accident that had forever changed his life.

It was not a thought he dwelt on. But that it had brought him single—wifeless—to this hour, he recognized. Why had the reaction of those girlish, simpering females so turned him against the opposite sex? Had popularity and massive doses of charm and overdoses of self-confidence been all there was to him, and, having it stripped away, had he been forced to find the man he should have been?

Well, time—and God—had taken care of it. As often before, Matthew mentally shook his head, marveling at the grace of a God who takes us at our worst and patiently and lovingly begins the task of making us into His image. Enough work had been done, he felt, enough ground gained for him to consider taking one more step—that of becoming a husband and, God willing, a father.

Matthew looked with satisfaction at his homestead: fields under cultivation, a meadow in which grazed a few cattle, a few outstanding horses, a sturdy barn and chicken coop, a granary and shed, a barn, and—his deepest source of contentment—his house. Set against the greenery and lushness of the bush, its windows twinkled invitingly at him as he rode toward it.

As he opened the door, for the first time Matthew was

struck by the silence, the emptiness, the *loneliness*. Where was the life? Where the laughter? Where the happy sharing, the eager welcome, the sounds of home? Where was the *love?*

Matthew, a disciplined man, checked his thoughts. Love? How could one rightly expect love from an arrangement such as Gussie had proposed?

But the laughter, the sharing, the welcome home—these could be forthcoming. Would they be enough? Matthew, a disciplined man, thought so.

3

"ARE YOU READY, DULCIE?"

"All set, Sister!"

"Well, come along then," Anna urged. "Time's getting away from us. It will be evening and milking time before we know it."

"Shaver's here—he'll take care of it!" Dulcie said rebukingly.

"Shaver—Shaver! Shaver can't do *everything*, Dulcie! We've had him take over far more now than is good for such a young man, so we can go gallivanting over to see Dovie all the time."

"He's as anxious for us to go as we are to go—you know that. As for the work, he seems to *thrive* on it. He came to us three years ago, when Digby and Dovie got married, just a raw kid. He's turning out to be a very handsome *man*."

"He is, isn't he?" Anna agreed fondly. "All those scones haven't hurt!"

"He does dote on them, doesn't he, Sister." It was a statement, not a question. "Poor dear—he was without a mother and good home cooking for . . . well, for all his *life*."

One of Shaver's first comments, on learning that his father was to marry Dovie Snodgrass and that he might, if he wished, move into the Snodgrass home and help the sisters run the farm, had been a heartfelt "Oh boy! Scones for tea every day!" His two new doting "aunts," Anna and Dulcie, had striven faithfully ever since to live up to his expectations.

With dear Papa dead and buried beside Mama in the Meridian cemetery, with no brother and with every relative far away in England, it was a brand-new experience indeed for the two spinsters to have a male "creature" around.

"I can't *imagine*," they speculated from time to time, "what it's like for Dovie." Digby, dear Dovie's husband, was twice the "male creature" Papa had been.

Dovie was no sooner married than she set her heart on having a baby. At her age! After the first shock had worn off, Anna and Dulcie not only accepted the idea but joined in the happy anticipation. Now, with two small bodies buried—one following the other in quick succession in the small graveyard Dovie had insisted should be on their own property—the expectations had faded into troubled concern. Dovie wouldn't listen to reason!

"You're too old, Sister!" they had told her.

"You've been happy for 40 years without a child!" they reminded her when she seemed bent on trying a third time.

"At least wait until you've gotten your *strength* back!"

Every argument had met with unexpected stubbornness on the part of Dovie.

And when Dulcie unfortunately made the suggestion "Maybe God doesn't *want* you to have a child, Dovie," she had almost cowered before the small furious explosion that was Dovie.

"How can you possibly know what God wants? For shame, Dulcie!"

"I only meant—maybe His will—"

"His will? His will? Didn't the Lord say, 'Suffer the little children to come unto me'?"

"But, Sister," Dulcie had defended feebly, "Jesus was speaking of *himself*. 'Come unto *me*,' He said!"

"Yes, and we are told to be like Him! And so I say it—I pray it! 'O God, suffer the little children to come unto *me!*'"

Dulcie had turned pale and crept away to whisper in half-frightened tones to Anna, "She's so—so *fierce* about it! I'm sure she isn't 'rightly dividing the word of truth,' Sister!"

Anna, wise as always, had soothed her younger sister. "We know, Sister, that God will do what is best."

But it seemed that God's best had ordained two small graves, and the sisters trembled for Dovie's faith should this third pregnancy be another disaster.

Dovie's time was very near now, and the sisters kept in close contact, ready to fly to her aid the moment Digby brought word. Dear Shaver's presence made it so much easier for them to get away from time to time.

Now Shaver had the horse hitched to the buggy, waiting at the door. Dulcie and Anna climbed in, waved a fond farewell to "dear Shaver," and rode over the small hills and through the verdant bush of a Wildrose spring to Dovie's.

"We really don't need all these sewing sessions, Sister," Anna said, glancing at the package of flannel in Dulcie's lap. "After all, we've been through this twice. I declare—we've made enough layette for triplets!"

"But it gives us an excuse to come," Dulcie explained. And, as usual with Dulcie, Anna was stumped on her reasoning. Why they couldn't just go on over to check on Dovie she couldn't imagine, without all this subterfuge, especially since Dovie herself knew exactly what they were up to.

Anna's bag was packed and ready. But her poor supply of equipment and medicines was sadly deficient to cope with trouble of a serious nature. Anna shuddered every time she remembered the terrible wound suffered by their neighbor Matthew Hunter and her feeling of help-lessness to do what was desperately needed.

The catalog, their chief source of supply for every-thing, offered pills and potions for such things as "A Cure to Stop the Drinking Habit" and made the ready promise of being "an excellent remedy for nervous headaches, neu-ralgia, sleeplessness, over brain work, depression follow-ing alcoholic excesses, and a fine bracer in the morning; and makes a pleasant drink when thirsty." They were go-ing to get you to take it—even drink it like water!—if it meant listing every ailment known to man . . . and woman!

Anna carried several elixirs she tried to put her trust in: "Seidlitz Powders—guaranteed to be genuine, pure, full strength (most of these powders bought from small stores are worthless from being kept too long)"; "neutralizing cordial, composed of rhubarb, peppermint, golden seal, cassia, etc.—a general corrector of the stomach, bowels, cholera morbus," and on and on.

Anna didn't suppose she would recognize cholera morbus if she met it face-to-face! In fact, she sometimes doubted the usefulness of all the advertised simples, nos-trums, draughts, restoratives, and decoctions. But people sick or in pain and desperate for relief would and did try anything. At least they felt something was being done for them; often Anna's presence alone was enough to turn the tide in an anxious situation.

For Dovie's confinement—beyond scissors, cat gut, uterine wafers, Dr. Barker's Blood Builder, and Dr. Wor-den's Female Pills for Weak Women—Anna had little to re-ly on. What, after all, were the vaunted Damina pills (pink for men, white for women)? What was Kennedy's Medical Discovery? As for Hamburg Breast Tea, how could it auto-matically control the flow of mother's milk, as promised, whether too fast or too slow, too rich or too thin?

Now, more than ever, Anna had grave doubts about the efficacy of some of her "cures." Perhaps the greatest blessing of all would be the small bottle of laudanum. But God grant that all would go well!

"Some day," Anna said as she turned the buggy out of the yard onto the road, "we'll all have access to Mr. Bell's wonderful telephone, and we won't have to make these trips just to get some reassurance."

"With a wire long enough to reach across the district? I'm sure!" Dulcie scoffed. "You might as well say we'll take wings and *fly* over!"

"You never can tell, Sister. Now take the Magic Lantern—wouldn't you just love to be entertained by the depiction of, say, Rip Van Winkle? Shaver says it's listed in the catalog: *Rip Van Winkle with the Children* and *Rip Van Winkle on the Mountains*."

"I don't know, Sister. I greatly fear it's a wicked invention. First thing you know, you'd be ordering and watching *Ten Nights in a Bar Room—Arrival at the Sickle and Sheaf* —what's that, Anna, but a saloon? And do you want a young mind like Shaver's polluted with *We Boys* or *Eve Before the Fall?* It gives me the shudders just to think about it!"

"Well, there's plenty of good if you make the right choices!" snapped Anna, not at all her usual controlled self, what with worry about Dovie heavy on her heart. "There's *Saul and the Witch of Endor, Flight into Egypt, Moses Saved—*"

"I greatly fear," Dulcie said with a sigh and a shake of the head, "it's a step in the wrong direction."

Anna turned stubborn. "What, then, is one to do, pray tell? These newfangled contraptions are here to stay, I'm sure. It will have to be—as I've already pointed out—a matter of *choices.* You may either choose 'The Dancing Skeleton—a new and striking effect,' or, on the other hand, you may wisely select 'Mount Vesuvius Erupting—throws out fire and smoke, very educational.'"

"You've been studying the catalog pretty closely yourself, I can see that!" Dulcie cried triumphantly.

"I think you may depend on my having a goodly supply of common sense, Sister," Anna responded quenchingly. "'Hold fast that which is good,' the Bible says, and I shall do just that!"

With such wisdom Dulcie couldn't argue. "Well," she finished, getting in the last word, "just don't forget to 'eschew evil.'"

The sisters, edgy with concern over their pregnant Dovie, concluded a rare and surprising wrangle—and felt no better when they were done than when they began.

With relief Anna turned the buggy into their sister's yard. No Dovie came to meet them. "Perhaps she's listening to the *gramophone*," Dulcie suggested pointedly, daring her sister to challenge the merits or demerits of this, another new contraption. Anna wisely bit her lip.

"Drop it, Dulcie," she said calmly, and Dulcie subsided.

They pushed open the door and stepped inside to find the house empty.

"Where could she be? We know she hasn't been jouncing around the country in the buggy these days."

Anna and Dulcie looked at each other, comprehension dawning in each pair of fading eyes—eyes that were now filling with anxiety.

In one accord they closed the door behind them. Together they crossed the farm yard, lifting dragging skirts, and entered a narrow path in the bush. Walking "Indian file," they continued until a clearing loomed ahead. Stepping into it from the dark, cool depths of the trees, their eyes went, again in one accord, to the small fenced area at the edge of the pasture. Surrounded by bush, the grave plot couldn't be seen until Anna and Dulcie stepped to the fence, erected of poles by Digby at Dovie's request.

"The rabbits can get in," Dovie had said, "and the birds, of course, and all the small creatures—the lovable ones."

At times the cows and horses stood looking over the top rail. And they often saw, as Dulcie and Anna did now, a lonely figure bent over the two small mounds.

Today Dovie was sitting between them, gently separating the wild flowers she had picked and laying them alternately on the graves.

Dovie was singing:

> *When He cometh, when He cometh*
> *To make up His jewels,*
> *All His jewels, precious jewels,*
> *His loved and His own.*

> *Like the stars of the morning,*
> *His bright crown adorning,*
> *They shall shine in their beauty,*
> *Bright gems for His crown.*

When she came to the final verse, two additional voices—husky, muted, loving—joined in the childish hymn they had sung in Sunday School across the years:

> *Little children, little children*
> *Who love their Redeemer*
> *Are the jewels, precious jewels,*
> *His loved and His own.*

And the two figures joined the kneeler to offer warm arms and gentle pats and to mingle tears and, eventually, prayers.

Then, through wet eyes, Dulcie and Anna saw for the first time the neat inscription that had been erected at the head of the graves.

SUFFER THE LITTLE CHILDREN TO COME UNTO ME

4

WITH SOME RELUCTANCE—BUT NOTING THE UN-
tidy appearance of the yardage and the two remaining minutes until the doors opened—Hannah moved to the
dress goods department and another mirror.

Karl Krueger, longtime associate of Morris Vaughn
and now Hannah's trusted manager, had raised a mild objection to the installation of another expensive mirror that
long-ago day.

"Why?" he had asked. "It's just yard goods, not clothing."

"Trust me, Karl," Morris Vaughn had said. "You're
aware, I think, that I know what's best for the Royal. The
trouble with you, Karl, is that you don't understand a certain basic principle—a man's need to appreciate feminine
beauty and a woman's need to feed that hunger. Isn't that
right, my dear?"

Amy, on hand for the momentous uncrating, admira-
tion, and hanging of the new acquisition, had laid aside the
bolt of black grenadine she had been fingering. At her elbow, Josie, the little sales clerk, was reciting nervously, under the cold eye of her employer: "It makes up beautifully
and looks rich and stylish when a lining of colored goods
is used underneath."

"And—," prompted Morris Vaughn coldly when Josie
faltered.

"And the effect is both striking and beautiful. This is just the material for warm weather wear, being of very light weight." Josie finished with a rush.

Morris shook his head over Amy's taste. "Go for the best, my dear," he tutted. "When will you learn quality?"

He chose a bolt of black Peau de Soie. "Pure silk," he said with satisfaction and unrolled it and held it up to his wife's peach-bloom cheek and studied the effect in the new mirror.

"Reversible—both sides look alike," the little clerk said, half chanting. "And the weave challenges the Duchess silks in popularity."

Morris waved the girl away. "I think I know my own goods, Miss Weaver," Morris said, and Josie, in confusion, retired.

Beauty-starved Hannah, by now a gangly teenager, had stroked a length of challis with brightly colored figures on a black background.

"Five cents a yard!" her father said distastefully, tweaking the offending goods from her hand. "And gaudy!"

Turning to the mirror, Morris studied his dashing self, his exquisite wife—and his self-effacing daughter, now looking at him with anxious eyes large in her pale face.

With a massive sigh, Morris asked, "How old is she?"

"Why, 16," Amy answered.

"Common sense would tell us," Morris spoke grimly, with a tightening of his lips, "that there is little or no possibility of the child finding a husband. As a good father, it's time I thought of her future." Then, under his breath but just loud enough for those nearby to hear, he said, "God unfortunately has not seen fit to bless me with a son." And as if making a pronouncement and the humble object of his remarks wasn't even present, he stated his conclusion: "Hannah will learn the business. The child is bright enough—it's only in the matter of style—and looks, and, er, *presence*, that she doesn't come up to snuff."

And Morris walked around Hannah, studying her as critically and dispassionately as though she were one of his own bolts of cloth goods—a particularly shoddy piece of goods—and therefore unacceptable.

"We'll make a place for her in the emporium. Now," Morris finally spoke to his daughter, "what do you think of that, eh?"

What Hannah had to say was surprising. Already confident that there would be no husband in the future and weary of her lessons, she agreed readily to the surprising suggestion, even eagerly, though she curbed it, knowing dimly that whenever she expressed a strong desire for something, it would most likely be criticized in favor of another plan—her father's plan.

Amy, less certain and almost as hesitant as uncertain, managed, "It might be wise to wait a year. Two years—when she's 18—"

More like her father than she knew, Hannah objected, stoutly and even vigorously pleading her case. Well practiced in the wifely art of compliancy, Amy gave in.

It meant a change of wardrobe from the childish gowns and plain pinafores. Of course, the store's merchandise was available within reason. Cautiously, of course, Hannah considered lizard cloth—all wool, very new and stylish; very fine taffeta silk—beautifully patterned, lined, and interlined; French organdy—a high grade novelty of the season; mohair Sicilian—with the appearance of silk, makes up beautifully; and more. She lingered over the exotic silks: very fancy black brocade silk, Dresden washable silk, plain black crystal silk, grosgrain silk, fancy illuminated novelty silk, all silk cannelle, and more.

Dizzy with the variety and the possibilities (and mistakenly thinking she was free to make her own choice), Hannah fed her imagination on bouclé, jacquard, lawn, madras, percale, challis. The emporium's vast gamut of supplies boggled the mind. What a day to be alive! What glorious merchandise—from England, the Orient, India, all parts of the globe—offering comfort, beauty, satisfaction!

But Hannah's lessons had been well learned. She chose for summer wear a plain, gray, ready-made Henrietta skirt ("This skirt is very desirable for elderly people, who prefer quality to show") and for winter wear "utilitarian serge."

Some faint desire for beauty would not die, and occasionally the young girl was tempted, in spite of all odds, to add one of the store's extravagantly beautiful "collarettes" to her costume. With their high necks, large square or pointed yokes, and the wide lacy frills that reached well beyond the natural shoulder line and flared over the bosom, they charmingly emphasized that particular portion of the female figure and narrowed the tightly cinched waist below. A silly temptation and soon conquered.

And so, in line with the lessons she had learned, Hannah chose Wearwell's high-grade linen collar. "There is the good collar that wears and the cheap collar that doesn't," the manufacturer warned, with the assurance: "We sell our good collars cheap."

Suitably gowned and scrupulously groomed, Hannah had developed a "style" of her own. As it evolved, Pansy and Gussie studied her and decided she had an "elegant look."

Hannah had scoffed. "Spare," had been her assessment. "A spare look."

"Well, whatever it is," both girls said, professing jealousy, "it's very attractive—on you," they added hastily and fingered their Spanish guipure lace and touched lovingly the moiré (watered) taffeta ribbon.

Pansy and Gussie were astute enough to recognize something else: For the first time in her life, Hannah was earning a certain amount of favor with her father. They gritted their teeth over it and wept at the thought of love and acceptance (well, not love perhaps) that had to be earned.

"She'd lick his boots," Pansy said sadly, "if it would get her some show of affection."

"He only approves now because she's good for business," Gussie added.

And in their own way the friends tried to make up for the lack, the terrible emptiness, in Hannah's life and, they were sure, in her heart. It was a loving responsibility they had assumed since childhood.

And then, suddenly, surprisingly, when Hannah was 20 and had been in the emporium four years, her parents died. First Amy, as a result of that winter's raging influenza epidemic, then Morris.

Hannah, numb with grief and shock, had found her salvation in the emporium, immersing herself in work. And her responsibilities were enormous. As her family's only survivor, Hannah fell heir to all her father's accumulation of wealth.

At Hannah's request, Karl Krueger had stepped into a place of leadership equal to her own. Only the fact that it was Vaughn money made a difference—to Karl, never to Hannah. Guiding Hannah, continuing to teach her what she needed to know to become one of the town's leading business people, Karl had proved his trustworthiness over and over; Hannah would indeed trust him with her life and certainly with her reputation and her investments.

Karl and Hannah were more than business associates; they were friends. Karl and Gretel, his wife, looked on Hannah as the daughter they never had.

And Pansy and Gussie had been there for her—until, in the natural course of events, each had fallen in love and married. Pansy and Buell Roop lived in Mayfair; Hannah played "auntie" to their two children. Gussie bade her friends an agonizing good-bye and left for the bush country of Saskatchewan with Henry Chapman, there to produce one baby and look for more. Ties with her beloved friends in Manitoba were maintained by correspondence.

Even now Gussie's last letter, arriving yesterday, crackled in the pocket of Hannah's neat, gray skirt.

Thinking of it, Hannah's thoughts whirled. Thinking of it, she turned at last for a frank study of herself. Leaning toward the "mirror of memories," she used the last few seconds before the doors opened to study herself honestly and (she thought) dispassionately.

Plain. That's all there was to it. Papa had been right. But when had she doubted it?

"You have a beautiful jaw line!" Pansy had argued from time to time, stemming the tide of Hannah's criticism of herself.

"Square," Hannah had corrected.

"Oval . . . round . . . square . . . pointed! Is one better than another?" Pansy asked.

"And my coloring—"

"Pure cream! Your complexion is pure cream. Now this high color of mine—ugh!"

"And my spots!" Gussie had wailed.

And the three girls fell into each other's arms, bemoaning their liabilities, real and imagined, and insisting the others were "perfect, just perfect!"

"At least, Hannah," Gussie had said, "you can't find anything wrong with your nose."

"So ordinary!" Hannah said, using the dreadful word.

"Now if you had a button for a nose, like me—" Pansy pinched the offending feature into a small peak and studied the effect in the looking glass in her hand.

But Pansy's button nose, Hannah reflected now, had been attractive to Buell. And Gussie's spots had faded, and her Henry had found her enchanting.

Hannah's ordinary nose, and eyes, and mouth, and her beautiful money had attracted Burt Nesselrode and his debts. There had been others, but their appearance had coincided too neatly with the newspaper's announcement of her inheritance to be taken seriously. Mason Gilbertson, for example, hadn't had the wit to pass one evening in her company without letting her know that his farm would blossom as the rose with better, costlier machinery. Sylvester Dill fancied himself the rightful heir to Morris Vaughn's place of honor in the community; Tedford Session . . .

It was all too dreary, and too humiliating, to dwell on.

But there was Delbert Bly. Hannah wasn't sure what attracted the minister, if attracted he was. Whatever the reason for his cautious pursuit, if pursuit it was, of his wealthiest parishioner, he was either unaffected by her money or—saddest of all possibilities—reluctant to take on the bodily source of it. At any rate, the relationship, if relationship it was, was lukewarm at best. As unsatisfactory as it was to Hannah, it seemed to satisfy Delbert, at least for the moment. Hannah, if she wanted more, was too dignified to pursue it.

Along the way, together with a definite "style" recognized by Gussie and Pansy and others, Hannah had developed a poise and dignity not suspected in the insecure child and uncertain youth.

Perhaps her responsible position, in the store and in the town, was at the root of it; she had simply grown to handle her expanding and more demanding obligations. Most likely it was the absence of an uncaring, critical father. While he was alive, Hannah had never ceased to care what he thought and to yearn silently, perhaps even in ignorance of it, for his approval.

The sharp ringing of the bell startled Hannah from her inspection and her reminiscences. No more satisfied with her reflection now than when she had seen herself through her father's eyes, she fled to the rear of the store and busied herself with the hosiery department. Around her, clerks were coming to attention, a buzz of voices approached as customers surged down the aisles, and the day, as always, was off to a busy start.

Being Saturday, and Sunday's flowers for the sanctuary much on his mind, Hannah wasn't surprised to see the large form of her pastor and *suitor* ambling toward her.

The most outstanding thing about the minister was that he was indeed large. Large and given to untidiness. "The dear man is so in need of a wife!" the women of the church clucked, casting knowing glances at Hannah if they were married and casting knowing glances toward Delbert if they were single.

He had been married. His wife, like Hannah's parents, had perished in the sweeping influenza of four years ago. Forty and childless, Delbert seemed in no hurry to change his status. But his attentions were directed doubtfully toward Hannah. If he was unmoved by any physical charms, he was also unmoved by the appeal of her money, and for that Hannah blessed him.

Behind his spectacles, Delbert's eyes warmed at the sight of Hannah. Feeling guilt for her small riffle of impatience because he was predictably concerned about the flowers, she greeted him a little more warmly than she might have otherwise.

"Good morning, Delbert!"

Delbert blinked, removed his hat, and smiled his slow smile. "Good morning, my, er, dear."

Delbert had obviously responded with what, for him, passed for effusion.

I wonder, Hannah thought suddenly, *what he would do if he knew about Gussie's letter*, and thought perversely, *It might just prod him into action.*

But did she want Delbert in action? And by being prodded? But the alternative—more months, perhaps, of his ponderous coming to some conclusion concerning remarriage—was unsettling.

"It's the flowers, isn't it, Delbert?" she said, now determined to force him into being decisive for once in his life.

"Why, yes," Delbert said, surprise on his broad, usually placid face. "How acute of you to foresee my need!"

"It doesn't take a lot of acuteness, Delbert," Hannah said with a sigh. It was beneath her, really, to bait the poor man.

"Of course it does, Hannah. And so like you! What a wonder you are, really!" And Delbert paused, blinking, obviously lost in the wonder of Hannah's perspicuity.

"The flowers?" she reminded, more gently. "Has Doramae slipped up again?" As deaconess in charge of the altar area, Hannah had delegated responsibility for the flowers to Doramae Brown. More often than not, Doramae forgot or, more likely, depended on the well-kept gardens of Vaughn House.

"That's it, I'm afraid. Not to criticize the dear soul, you understand. Not everyone is as dependable as you, I'm afraid."

Delbert, it seemed to an unusually critical Hannah, was afraid too often.

"Fear not, O Delbert," she caroled and immediately equated her flippancy to the letter in her pocket. Was she already feeling independent of Delbert Bly? She had the grace to blush when Delbert looked—not annoyed, but taken aback.

"What I mean is—," she continued quickly, "I'll see to them."

"Oh, thank you!" Delbert's relief was obvious. "Now, while I'm here—perhaps I may look at the hosiery. Mine seem to have developed holes at an alarming rate. Of course," he added thoughtfully, which was about Hannah's only clue to the fact that he was considering the pros and cons of marriage, "they never get mended."

A bubble of something close to hysteria threatened Hannah's composure as she swallowed what seemed like, at the moment, the only reasonable retort for a minister of Delbert's gravity: "What—holey socks?"

Slightly overcome with her strange lack of decorum and proper respect for a reverend and her suitor, she collected herself and managed, "How about these?" and pointed to a new display of fancy, silk, embroidered socks.

Too late she noticed the assortment of colors and the fancy figures and dots embroidered in silk.

Delbert seemed to blanch. "I'm afraid not," he said stiffly, obviously now not at all sure he should discuss anything as intimate as footwear with a female.

"Fear not, O Delbert," Hannah said, but silently, and took Delbert's elbow discreetly and turned him toward the "men's fast, black, cotton half hose." Clearly suitable for a man of the cloth, these promised to be "full seamless, fine quality with spliced heels and toes and fine elastic ribbed tops."

"I say!" Delbert brightened, "these are marked half price!"

Dear Delbert—he *could* use a little extra money. Hannah, by now sensitive to the matter of her wealth, squelched the idea as unworthy of the minister's motive as he made reference to his meager salary.

"Perhaps a male clerk—," Hannah was suggesting with a return to her usually sensitive response to Delbert's needs.

"Of course!" Delbert obviously felt a sense of relief.

Escaping, Hannah sought the seclusion of her office. Seated in her comfortable chair at her desk, she took a deep breath, stilling what seemed to be a tumultuous beating of her heart, and drew Gussie's letter from her pocket.

Dear Hannah:

Don't stop reading until you hear me out!

Knowing me across the years at home, and now here as intimately as you do through reams and reams of correspondence, you already suspect that I'm going to be SERIOUS!

I'll not beat around the bush (no pun intended!).

The purpose of this letter is to introduce you to one Matthew Hunter. You've heard me mention him; he's often here for dinner or supper. And that's because he's a BACHELOR.

Matthew is in his middle 30s, has his own place, and is doing well. And he is LOOKING FOR A WIFE. Well, not looking exactly, but WILLING. Well, that, too, may be an exaggeration. He is not your Burt Nesselrode type of man—pushy. Neither is he your Delbert Bly type—reluctant.

He is such a dear, in fact, that he deserves the very best. And the very best is YOU, Hannah.

Dear Gussie, Hannah thought, *so loyal to me! If she so misreads me, how far wrong is she on this bush country acquaintance?* But Gussie answered that too:

Now, Hannah, you think I exaggerate your qualities, so I want to assure you that I have told Matthew only that you are my dear friend and AVAILABLE (say you are! in spite of Delbert!). By the same token you can be equally sure I am not painting an unrealistic picture of Matthew. He is a very attractive man, and he is AVAILABLE.

Why, you ask, if he is all that worthy, isn't he married? To understand you need only recall that Henry had to come out of the bush to find *me*. The lack of females here is legendary. Hosts of single men have flooded the territories in search of land; even the most unlikely females have been grabbed up. Matthew is showing great CIRCUMSPECTION in trusting me in this regard. I am touched at his trust in my opinion.

Your opinion of me, dear Gussie, Hannah thought wryly, *has ever been prejudiced because of your love for me. The man probably expects a paragon of beauty, poise, and ability.*

I'm just asking that you allow Matthew to WRITE to you. But I will say this: Men here in the backwoods haven't got time for a lot of traditional courting. Some even advertise for a wife; Matthew won't do that. But he is willing to trust my judgment. Now how about you? Put bluntly—what have you got to lose? Only Delbert and a life so PREDICTABLE that you know each morning what the day will bring forth. You are wasted in humdrum Mayfair! Don't you secretly long for more excitement than that? Isn't there something of the pioneer in you? Doesn't life on the frontier challenge you? Oh, Hannah, say YES!

Matthew is no Sunday suitor; he isn't in this to play parlor games. There will be no hand-kissing and no double-talk such as traditional Victorian lovers often do. This could have SERIOUS CONSEQUENCES and quickly! Life here in the bush may be rough, but it is honest. And it is REAL, Hannah. Please say Matthew may write.

Henry sends love or would if he knew I was writing.

Ever your loving,
Gussie

Folding the letter, Hannah raised her eyes to the glass-windowed door leading from her office to the store beyond. She could see the shadowy familiar figures going about their familiar tasks. A little farther away Delbert was deliberating about what socks to buy; these, too, would need mending in the days ahead. And replacing, and mending . . .

Beyond the store stretched streets she had walked every year of her life; every crack in the sidewalks was known to her by heart.

Her imagination saw, next, the ornate front door of Vaughn House opening to its rich furnishings. Her father's house. What sort of person would she be away from its cloying, stifling influence? What could she become away from the routine of Vaughn's Royal Emporium? What vistas did life offer in a new setting, in the rough, honest, and real setting of the frontier?

Like a drowning man offered a fresh gulp of air, Hannah's heart, parched for emotion, reached passionately for the tantalizing breath of reality opening to her—and having opened, could never be closed again. The glimpse through that door would follow her down through her dull days, across her stereotyped years, and would accompany her to the grave—a grave already bought and paid for, at the side of her father and mother.

The allurement of the bush, before she ever saw it or breathed its aroma, captured her. A passion to experience life left her shaken. If it meant embracing Matthew Hunter—the reality as well as the abstraction—so be it.

Lifting a sheet of paper from the desk drawer and taking up her pen, Hannah wrote swiftly, decisively:

Dear Gussie:

Your letter at hand.

Tell your Matthew to write. Why not?

Ever your friend,

Hannah

P.S. Do not—under any circumstances—tell him about the money.

THE SMALL GIRL, BITING HER LIP AND FROWNING
with the effort of her concentration, lifted the heavy
iron skillet with both hands—hands that were far too
workworn for her age, hands that bore far too many scars
for someone 10 years old, hands that had experienced life
far more harshly than they should have and tackled tasks
far too difficult.

There was no breeze to carry the fire's smoke toward
the somewhat grimy face straightening from its heat, carefully turning toward the table set at the side of the bedraggled prairie schooner. The wagon seemed to droop wearily
toward the grasses that browned in the heat of the early-
morning sun.

The thin shoulder blades bunched under the faded
dress as Holly Carroll strained to set the skillet on the
table. And the little face lit with pleasure when it was ac-
complished.

"Da," she called, "breakfast's ready! Neddy—soup's
on!"

"Soup?" There was an eagerness in the little boy's
voice as he came scampering from a distant hillock at the
sound of his sister's call. "Oh boy!"

"Not really truly soup, Neddy," Holly said ruefully.
"That's just a—a figger of speech. Mama said it—don't you
remember?"

"Aw!" Neddy's disappointment was obvious.

"Perhaps tomorrow," Edward Carroll said as he approached the fire area. "Come, Neddy—let's not forget our manners. There's water to wash our hands even if there isn't enough for an all-over bath. We should be able to indulge ourselves in that tonight. On my way home, I'll go by the creek in the coulee and fill the barrels. You have enough for the day, Holly?"

"Yes, Da. And enough to wash the dishes. And I'll pour the water on my garden when I'm done with dinner."

Holly cast an anxious glance toward a small, scraggly plant. Its leaf formation and its scanty thorns hinted at its being a rosebush, probably a poor specimen of the wild rose that bloomed so profusely across the territories in good years.

"I'll build a shade over it before I go," her father said, noting the concern on the child's face. So loving of beauty and so starved for it, the rose symbolized what her heart craved and what she missed so much.

But there was another reason, and Ed Carroll's mouth softened momentarily.

Back on the prairie, at the edge of the town straggling to obtain a foothold, a freshly heaped mound of sod marked the last resting place of his wife, his Rose.

"Yes," he said softly, "I'll give it some shade. And when I get back tonight with the water, we'll give it a good drink."

Edward and Neddy, his namesake, pulled rough stools up to the equally rough table, bowed their heads, and the elder male prayed, "For what we are about to receive, O Lord, make us truly thankful."

Neddy looked mutinous, as though he were having a hard time being "truly" thankful for the food Holly was scooping into his bowl.

"Mush again!" he sighed.

"Soup tomorrow," his father promised, and Neddy

brightened. "I'll stop at the store when I'm finished at the barn raising."

This trip, not often made, would accomplish several things—his duty toward a distant neighbor who was ready to erect a barn, the purchase of a few groceries, and filling the empty barrels before they shrank beyond use in the hot sun.

Neddy looked wistful as his father finished his breakfast—fried mush with a dribbling of syrup over it (there was no milk)—and asked, "Can I go, Da?"

"You wouldn't enjoy it today, Neddy," Edward Carroll answered. "It's a long, hot trip—dusty and slow—and there are no children to play with, and no shade. You'd be under Mrs. Whipple's feet in their shanty all day. You'd hate that."

"And so would Mrs. Whipple," Holly, the little "housewife," said wisely. "Tell you what, Neddy—we'll fix up a game of checkers, and I'll teach you to play."

Neddy's four-year-old face, brown and chapped under his mop of red-gold curls, brightened.

"Da," Holly said softly, turning to her father as he laid aside his spoon and prepared to leave the table, "will you go by and see Mama?"

"Mama's grave, Holly. Not today, Honey. I won't be out in that direction. Next time I go, you can go along."

"And maybe my bush will have a rose by then! I'll take it and give it to Mama. She'll love that!"

"Yes, Honey, she will." Edward's voice was unsteady. He bent and kissed the small face, so like a rose itself, a dusky, sun-blessed rose, and suggested that Neddy come help him hitch up.

Neddy scampered away with his father to round up the team from their usual fare of prairie grasses. His father hoisted the boy onto the back of a horse and led it toward the crude shelter that passed for a temporary barn and the harness hanging there.

Holly made a careful pan of suds for the spoons and

bowls, poured the water into the skillet, scrubbed it with a handful of dried, bunched grass as she had seen her mother do on countless occasions as they trekked across the prairies, always heading toward what Mama dreamily called "the parkland." The parkland and roses. The vision had inspired Mama's songs, it had threaded itself through her bedtime stories, it had lifted her feet with hope through mile after mile of endless prairie.

Like a beacon, the parkland and the roses had beckoned Mama. And to think the fever had taken her, almost within sight of her goal.

"Why are we stopping here?" had not been necessary to ask when their father pulled the wagon into the small hollow, unhitched, and unloaded. Mama was, after all, a few miles away. Da couldn't bear to leave her. Not yet.

And when he doggedly set to work to establish some kind of permanent living quarters, Holly settled for the prairie. For now.

But her mother's dreams lived in Holly's heart. Often she took the short walk to the small promontory that was the highest peak on the rolling prairie. Turning her gaze northward, she could fancy she saw a faint, dark line. It wasn't an impossible dream. "Yes," Edward had said, "it's right over there."

So near, and yet so far.

Not that the "really truly" bush started there, a dozen miles away, but the terrain and the landscape began its slow and significant change. To the knowing heart, it kindled expectations and teased of greener, much greener, pastures.

Holly poured the dishwater around the struggling bush that had been dug and carefully transported from the coulee, with its water and its greenery.

"I hope the soap isn't hurting it," the child thought anxiously. There were many other things she could have done with the few cupsful of the precious liquid: She and

Neddy could have washed in it at noon; she might have managed to rinse out an item or two of clothing. But Da would bring water tonight, and she and Neddy could put up with dusty faces and dirty hands for a few more hours. And the clothes would wait another day.

Edward drew his little daughter to him, hugged her for a few seconds, did the same with his son, and swung himself into the wagon. The schooner's canvas top and ribs had been removed. The ribs would make the poles for their roof, and the canvas, now covering their household goods, would cover the poles before the sod was put on.

"That way," Edward explained to the children, "we won't have water and mud falling through, like most soddies do. We'll have a nice ceiling!"

And the children, envisioning it, nodded.

It would not be a true soddy. Because of the small hillock, their home would be more rightly termed a dugout. Edward was wearily engaged in digging into the hillside, scooping out a living space, and cutting and digging squares of sod for three walls; the hillside would make the fourth. And over all would stretch the wagon's canvas.

Neighbors, though distant, had been sympathetic, attending the burial that had to be done quickly because of the hot weather and because their hearts—and in some cases their memories—were stirred by the stunned face of the man and the bewildered look on the faces of the two children. Now Edward was to take the day off to help one of them in his barn raising; neighbors in turn would trundle across the prairie to offer what help they could from time to time, and what encouragement.

With her hand on her brother's shoulder, Holly watched the wagon rattle away.

"Da!" she shouted, and her father turned his head. "Bring wood for the fire!"

Edward Carroll nodded and waved. Holly's palms were sore and red from the everlasting twisting of prairie grasses to feed the small fire necessary to cook their meals. While at the creek for water, Edward would search the coulee for dry wood. It promised to be a very busy day. Even now the heat was almost unbearable; his shirt, damp across his back, soon dried in the beating rays of a sun curving the vast prairie world in its relentless summer arc.

If Holly's final wave was accompanied by anything more, the sound was lost in the rattle of his cargo.

When Edward Carroll, in his sorrow and grief and bowed with a weariness beyond enduring, had decided to stay on the prairie, there was another reason: He had run out of resources. Oh, perhaps there was enough to scrape together the cost of the filing fee he would have to pay to obtain his land grant farther north, where Rose's heart, in particular, had fixed with longing. But their supplies were low; wherever they settled, life would be almost impossibly hard, at least for a few years. Edward's courage, along with his dreams, had all but flickered out. It was simpler, some way, to "drop anchor" and let the prairie schooner come to port—a dry and dusty port—here to rest awhile, allow time for his tipping world to right itself, and to regain his dwindled courage for the mammoth task of homesteading.

Too late in the season to do anything about a crop—he had, after all, no fields plowed and no machinery—Edward and the children had scoured the prairies for buffalo bones to sell. Although the buffalo themselves had disappeared some years previously, abruptly and irrevocably, their bones remained, whitening the prairies. With no hope of a green crop this year, Edward settled for the white and the cash obtained in town when the bones were sold, to be shipped to American sugar refineries.

Now he trundled off to town, his harvest of bones rattling in the bottom of his wagon. Flour, sugar, beans, perhaps a piece of meat. Definitely meat! Hadn't he promised soup? Without a hope of fresh vegetables, except perhaps onions and potatoes, even a decent stew seemed impossible.

Holly, only 10, did her best, bless her! Edward's eyes misted as he remembered again the incredulity with which she had received from his hand the first gophers and the gameness with which she had stewed them.

Yes, he would bring home some beef. Even as he decided, he knew the vicious heat, with no ice house or even a deep well in which to keep anything, would turn the meat quickly rotten. Most likely it was oatmeal he should concentrate on—again.

Turning, he caught a final glimpse of his camp—half-finished dugout, a pile of canvas-covered goods, one small fire, and two tiny figures—slowly fading into specks in the immensity of the prairie.

To some, the prairie's vastness was impelling, even compelling to those used to it. Without windbreaks, though, there was no protection from the blistering heat that caused the distant figures to dance crazily. In winter, however, a line would need to be strung from house to barn if he were to survive the storms.

Women, Edward knew, went out of their minds with the loneliness, the hopelessness, the deprivations, and with watching at the side of a rude sod shack for a glimpse of her man returning while he was still far, far away. Could Holly cope? Edward prayed she might and stifled the terrible guilt he felt for trapping her in a situation far beyond her abilities to handle. Yes, he gritted savagely, he'd bring meat home tonight if it killed him!

Holly turned from watching her father disappear over the far horizon like an ant falling over the lip of the world. The silence was complete; at the moment there was no meadowlark, no insect chirp, and, of course, no human voice. Not even a cow's bawl or a dog's bark. She shivered and clutched more tightly the small hand holding hers.

Looking down at the face of her brother, seeing her fears reflected there and needing to banish them, she knelt quickly in the drying grass, gathered him into her arms, and rocked him back and forth, back and forth, as she had seen Mama do many times. Gradually the stiff little form relaxed.

"Now," she said, her voice no more than a pin's drop in the vast bowl of the heavens, "we were going to play checkers, weren't we?"

"But I don't know how, Sissy."

"You can learn, just like I learned from Mama. Come on now—we'll have to make us some checkers."

"What are checkers?" Neddy was interested, his fears fading. But Holly knew they had only receded, to stand just out of sight, waiting for night and dream time.

Quickly she said, "A real checker is called a man, and it's moved around on a checkerboard. We don't have a board, and we don't have the men, Neddy, so we'll have to see what we can invent. Won't that be fun?"

Neddy looked around doubtfully. Nothing but windswept grass and, at their backs, the dugout, just a hole in a hill.

"Now come on," Holly was urging. "Back over here we threw the broken pieces of the teapot. It was all in smithereens when we came to unpacking—remember?"

"Why do we want broken glass?"

"It will do very nicely for men. See? Here's a perfect little piece with a pretty blue cornflower on it. And another—"

"Here's more!" shouted Neddy, already into the spirit of the game.

Holly gathered up a corner of her dress and dropped the chinaware into it. When she felt they had enough, they turned to hunting tiny pebbles. "Try to get them about the same size," she directed, and soon the extra weight sagged the dress, and they turned toward home base—a campfire, a pile of household goods, and a cave in the side of a hillock.

There was no board and, if they'd had one, nothing with which to mark squares. Pondering the problem, Holly reflected, "Where there's a will there's a way, Neddy. Mama always said so."

"What's a will, Sissy?"

"It's a—a—an idea. And I have one."

Holly looked around for a twig or piece of wood—all had been burned.

"I need to make marks in the dirt, Neddy—"

"A spoon?" Neddy suggested, and Holly crowed with praise for his cleverness.

Digging the spoon from a box and clutching her bundle of broken china and pebbles, Holly made for the small shade inside the hollowed-out hillside.

"See, Neddy? It will be cool here but still bright enough to see."

With the spoon handle Holly painstakingly marked a checkerboard in the dirt. Neddy was impressed.

"Now, Neddy, you get to choose which men you want—the china or the pebbles."

After a great deal of consideration, weighing them in his hand, checking out the flowers and examining the sharp edges, he decided. "You should have the pretty ones, Sissy. I know you like pretty things." And Neddy scooped the pebbles from the ground where Holly had put them and, at her instruction, placed them in rows on the checkerboard.

Soon they were lost in the intricacies of moving, jumping, and crowning their men. The morning passed, with only the occasional cry of a bird or riffle of a hot wind to divert their attention.

At noon Holly doled the remainder of the porridge—as warm from the sun as it had been, earlier, from the fire—and the children ate, drinking sparingly of the equally warm water.

Neddy's eyes were heavy. *He's still just a baby, really,* Holly thought with the mothering instinct that had been born at the death of her mother.

"Come, Neddy," she said gently and led the little boy back to the only shade the whole entire world provided. There he cuddled against her side.

"Sing Nonee-no," he demanded.

And Holly, raised on the simple, hypnotic melody, sang the nearly wordless little refrain over and over until Neddy's blue eyes drooped and finally closed in sleep. The thin sound of the comforting strain, passed from mother to child for generations, worked its magic here on the lonely prairie as it had in sturdy houses in the eastern part of this great country and across an ocean in forgotten domiciles of all qualities and sizes; wherever a mother's love existed and a childish ear listened, it had been sung. With Rose in her grave—hidden silently away and eventually to be forgotten in all but the memories of two small children—the song lived on.

Alone with her song and her memories, Holly, too, closed her eyes and slept.

Some distant sound woke her. "Da!" But the sun was still high and hot.

Stepping out into the brilliance of the afternoon, Holly shaded her eyes and watched the approach of her father's team and the decrepit wagon.

"Dada!"

Gathering up her skirt, Holly ran toward the rig, regardless of dust and heat.

"Whoa!" The wagon pulled to a stop. Shading her eyes against the light, Holly reached a hand up, ready to step onto the hub and be pulled up onto the seat.

There was no hand. And the dry half-cough from the driver of the team was a strange sound to the child. As she squinted her eyes, her gaze moved quickly to take in the team—it was Da's. The wagon—she recognized the weather-warped and silvered boards. But the voice—

The voice . . . the voice . . . was not Da's.

6

"LOOK HERE, GERRY. WHAT DO YOU THINK OF these?" Elva Victor's needle-pricked finger pointed to the catalog and the page titled "Men's Linen Collars and Cuffs."

Gerald Victor, struggling mightily with a collar button, bent over the array of "newest, nobbiest, and best styles of the season."

"Nobby?" questioned the minister.

"That means smart, of the first quality or style. Surely a man of your education knows that!"

"I don't know much about style anymore—that's for sure," Gerald said ruefully. "My credentials don't cover what's proper for outward adorning. Sometimes I don't do too well on the meek and quiet spirit, which is the adorning of the hidden man of the heart, either. Now this collar button, for instance! It would drive a saint to desperation!"

With a smile Ellie rose from her chair at the side of the table where she had been considering placing an order for shirt collars for her husband and dealt with the stubborn button.

"The trouble is," she explained, "I have to starch these threadbare collars within an inch of their lives if they are to hold up for one more wearing! I can manage making shirts"—Ellie held up the injured finger—"but collars are beyond me! Mine always turn out bunched or crooked.

They *are* the part that shows, and I've caught Dolly—Sister Trimble, that is—looking at yours critically."

"Let her look! As long as they're clean—"

"They don't stay that way very long. You know you use two a day sometimes. Is it necessary to wear a collar today? You're only going to Meridian, for heaven's sake!"

"I'm going to stop to see Dovie and Digby along the way. Her time is getting close, and I know how anxious she is, though she tries to hide it."

"We're all anxious—everyone in Wildrose. Things have just got to go well in this confinement. Two dead babies, Gerry, in about two years! She'll appreciate some extra prayers."

"Help me with this?" Gerry held up the "Gentlemen's Silk Bow Tie" the children had ordered for their father for Christmas. Black, of course, "made from the remnants of high-grade ties," costing six cents, but they would have "cost a quarter in any retail store." Emmie and Buddy had been particularly drawn by the sentence: "There is nothing old or off-color; every one is as handsome as can be." Tie or wearer? It mattered not.

They were not the only ones to think Gerald Victor was handsome in his tie "with shield for turn-down collar." Ellie turned the collar down now, patted the result, stood on tiptoe and kissed the gentle face above it, and returned to her study of the catalog.

"Not those celluloid things," Gerald warned.

"They come in Clerical, Royal, Imperial, Sterling, and Excelsior styles," Ellie teased.

"Next thing would be celluloid cuffs—"

"The Albert, Edmund, Mortimer, Warwick, and Clarence."

"And celluloid shirt fronts—"

"This is fascinating, Gerry. At the bottom of many pages there is an added note. See?—right here along the bottom, in dark print. Words of wisdom I never noticed before."

"Mmmmm." Gerald was lacing his ankle-high shoes, which, Ellie knew, were made over a Bull Dog last, boasted a heavy pebbled surface, and had been warranted "crack proof."

"This says: 'You will gain the lasting gratitude of your neighbor if you will persuade him to send for our catalog.'"

Gerry was winding his pocket watch, a parting gift from his father when he (Gerry) had departed the "civilized" world for a church in the bush country.

"And listen to this, Gerry—at the bottom of a page of shoes it says, 'If by any reason you get a pair of shoes that do not fit, don't get mad. The chances are that you gave the wrong size. We guard carefully against errors on our part.' Isn't that nice to know, Gerry? Nice to know one can rely on such honest practices—"

"No celluloid!"

Gerald Victor kissed the cheek bent in earnest concentration over the "wish book" and turned to sift through the items on the bureau top.

Ellie, not to be sidetracked, hadn't read anything so entertaining in a long time. "'If you don't need enough goods to make a freight order,'" she read, "'perhaps your neighbor does, and you can send together.' What a good suggestion! And this—'In ordering suits for boys, be sure to state age of boy and say whether large or small for his age.' And listen to this—'When you buy from us you are sure of the latest styles, such as prevail in large cities. Your local milliner does the best she can, but the prices are double those we name.' Now I doubt that, Gerry. Our local milliner makes sun bonnets! And from scraps . . . Gerry? Gerry?"

But Gerry wasn't listening. Turning back to the collar and cuff page, Ellie murmured, "Now let's see—'Perfect fitting, all linen, 4-ply, with handmade button holes and double stitching.' But $1.40 a dozen!" And Ellie studied her sore finger and rethought her extravagance in ordering ready-made after all.

"Perhaps I should just make them—"

"Here it is! I thought I must have thrown it out."

"Thrown what out, Gerry?"

"This letter from Rose Carroll. Goodness knows it's lain here long enough—"

"Your uncle's second wife's niece—"

"Something like that. I really don't have it figured out. Uncle Mack is dead, of course, and so are his second and third wives—"

"And, of course, his first."

Gerald Victor flashed his wife a surprised look, to be met by her laughing face.

"Goose!" he said. "He wasn't as blessed as I am. At any rate, Ellie, it's been several months since this niece-in-law—or whoever she was to Uncle Mack—wrote to tell me she had found my name and address among family effects and wanted information about homesteading in this area."

"You answered right away, as I remember."

"But I haven't heard anything more. If she and her family started out upon getting my letter, they could be in the area by now. Strange, though, that I never heard another word from her."

"Maybe she'll just turn up someday. Or maybe her letter was lost—many are, we know."

"Well," Gerry said, crumpling the letter and dropping it into the wastebasket, "I wouldn't know this Rose Carroll if I met her face-to-face."

"They may have found a suitable homestead, or even a job, somewhere along the way."

"Could be. I doubt I'll ever hear from her again. Well, I'm off to Meridian and a call on Dovie."

＊　＊　＊

It was an anxious-eyed Digby who stepped off the porch and went to the buggy to meet the minister.

"Hello, Brother Victor—I'm glad to see you."

"Something wrong, Digby?"

Gerald Victor studied his parishioner's face as his foot found the small iron step, and he leaped from it to the ground.

"No, no! That is—maybe. There are signs—and it's too early. But perhaps not too early. These little ones tend to come when they make up their minds—"

Digby, usually a man of action rather than words, stumbled through the recitation.

"The truth is, Gerald—I'm worried. It's because of the other two times, you see—"

"And Dovie—how is she doing?"

"Bravely. But come on in. She'll be glad to see you. If I know Dovie, she'll have the kettle on for tea."

About to enter the house, Digby put a hand on the minister's arm, paused, and said in a low voice, "Dovie's got some kind of a bee in her bonnet. For such a pliable little thing, she's showing unusual—" Digby was at a loss for words.

"I guess 'persistence' would be the word," Digby said. "Maybe you can talk her into a little more—caution."

"Caution, Digby?"

"Where the Word of God is concerned. She has set her heart—and her head—on a certain portion, and Gerry— she's determined it says something other than it does!"

Dovie seemed her usual cheery, talkative self, to her pastor.

"If I'd only known—," she clucked, "I'd have had *scones* for you!"

All of Wildrose benefited from the Snodgrass ritual carried over from their English heritage.

"It's my own fault!" her pastor admitted. "But these will do nicely."

Dovie, while Digby and Gerald had talked outside, had poured the tea and brought out a plate of matrimonial cakes. The date filling was a rare treat, and her pastor fell to eating with a will.

Finally, brushing oatmeal crumbs from his vest, he asked, "Well, Dovie, how are you doing?"

"Very well," Dovie said serenely.

"I'm glad," her pastor said gently. "Everyone else, it seems, is concerned for you. Is there some, ah, reason for this peace? The Lord, I presume."

"You know how you are always encouraging us to be like Jesus?"

"Yes, of course!"

"You know you tell us to take Him at His word?"

"I'm gratified to see someone is listening."

"And you know that Jesus said, 'He that believeth on me, the works that I do shall he do also'?"

Gerald was becoming a little uneasy. "Yes," he said slowly, "I know that scripture."

"Well," Dovie said triumphantly, "there you are!"

"Just where is that, Dovie?" her pastor asked cautiously, and Digby shifted uneasily.

In response, Dovie quoted some unknown poet:

> If Jesus is the Word exhibited,
> And with the blessed Word I'm tenanted,
> May I not boldly speak what He has said?

Dovie was masterfully weaving a web around her pastor. Now her bright eyes challenged him to refute, or acknowledge, the truth of what she was saying.

If I knew where she was going with this, Gerald thought. *If Digby had clued me in a little more.*

"Well," he offered now, "it depends on what it was He said."

"You mean we can't believe *everything* He said?"

"No—I'm not saying that. Of course, we can—"

"Or that we can't follow His example in *everything*?"

"Now, Dovie," Gerald said, getting a slight grip on the situation, "let's consider His invitation to Peter to walk on water. Was that an open invitation to everyone?"

"But if He spoke it to *me*, I could."

"Well, yes." Gerald felt the trap tightening.

"And haven't you told us to *appropriate* the promises?"

"I have."

"So!" Dovie sat back, her face aglow with her victory.

"Just what scripture are you appropriating, Dovie?" Gerald asked, while Digby lowered his head, his face reflecting his distress.

"'Suffer the little children to come unto me,'" Dovie said promptly.

"Dovie," Gerald said, his duty clear at last. "Jesus was calling little children to *himself*."

"If Jesus said it, *I* can say it," Dovie said, setting her round little jaw.

Digby looked at his pastor helplessly.

"Dovie, I have to be honest with you. You are setting yourself up for a terrible disappointment if anything should, God forbid, go wrong. There are other wonderful promises of His help, His grace, His presence—"

"But I'm appropriating that one about the children."

Looking at her—eyes wide and earnest, trust written on her face puffed with her pregnancy—her pastor could not bring himself to wipe out that bright hope.

"Ah, Dovie," he said, and it was almost a groan, "what can I tell you? If God has quickened a scripture to you, . . . then"—a beading of perspiration appeared on Gerald's brow—"stand on it."

Digby looked startled then dismayed. Gerald, in a daze, offered a stumbling prayer, said his good-byes, and left.

"What a spot to be in!" he said miserably to Ellie when he had poured out the account to her.

"But Gerry—what if this baby, like the others, dies?"

"We shall just have to pray—and pray hard!—that it doesn't."

If God wasn't on the line, the pastor was.

7

THE SKY WAS A BLUE COVERLET, WHITE-TUFTED, when Gussie put Hanky in the red wagon and trundled down the bush-bound road toward the Ivey farm. Still considering herself a newcomer to Wildrose, Gussie could not take for granted what the weary homesteader may have long since ceased to bless, finding instead a threat to the crop in the rainless sky or a threat to the hay when the refreshing downpour occurred.

Spring—delicious, aroma-saturated after an odorless, snowbound winter, longed for and rejoiced in—could so quickly turn ugly and disappear under an untimely snowfall. And the growing season of barely 100 days could be cruelly cut short by an early snowfall. The bush itself, verdant and lovely, lost its charm before the relentless onslaught of ax and grub hoe and the absolute need to clear enough of it to make a living.

Dimly knowing these things, having heard them often enough, Gussie was an advocate of "whatsoever things are lovely . . . if there be any virtue, and if there be any praise, think on these things."

Today this was not hard to do. Birds flashed around, filling the sky and bush with incredible bursts of song. Wildflowers, most of which she couldn't name, threaded the grasses. And, just as she remembered, one patch of roadside was matted with wild strawberry vines. Ready for a rest from the awkward pull of the small wagon, Gussie lifted Hanky to the ground, and together they spent a happy few minutes picking and eating the brilliant, sweet gems.

When they pulled into the Ivey clearing, it was to find Dovie, hands on hips, back rigidly stiff, stomach bulging, walking the rows of her garden.

"Frustrated, Dovie?" Gussie greeted with understanding.

Dovie laughed. "The potato bugs are sticking out their tongues at me. But their days are numbered!"

Dovie rubbed the small of her back with one hand. "It won't be long now, Gussie."

"Can I pick something for you?" Gussie asked.

"I was looking longingly at the lettuce," Dovie said. "Seems I can't get enough fresh stuff."

"It was a long winter."

Between selecting choice lettuce leaves and riding herd on a rambunctious Hanky who was bent on having a salad of his own making, Gussie and Dovie talked.

"Truly—how are you?" Gussie asked.

Dovie hesitated. Then, "Truly—fair. There are enough signs just like the last two times to cause me some concern, but there are encouraging things too. For one thing, I've carried this baby longer than the others. Truly—I'm at peace. Truly—I expect everything to be all right."

"That has to be God-given," Gussie said. "An example of the peace that passes understanding."

With Dovie carrying the lettuce and Gussie leading a protesting Hanky, the two friends made their way to the house and the simmering kettle. Gussie waved to Digby when he stepped from the shadow of the barn and looked toward the sound of the voices.

"He's never very far away these days," Dovie said, "except perhaps when Dulcie and Anna come spend the day with me. Then he scoots off to the meadow or field or somewhere else, getting all sorts of things done."

"What a loving, caring man he is!"

"I'm so blessed, Gussie. And to think I almost missed all the joy—I was single a long time. Now with Digby *and* a family of my own—who could ask for more? God has been so good to me."

"And to me," her friend agreed soberly, her thoughts on an equally loving and caring husband and precious family.

Thinking of this particular blessing, Gussie's thoughts turned naturally to her friend Hannah. Hannah, so straight and true, so capable and so kind—Gussie's evaluation of her distant friend went on and on. Went on to include: Hannah—so cheated; Hannah with her possessions and her money—so robbed of the *normal* joys of life. And Gussie fondled Hanky's curls, pressed her hand to her unborn child, and thought of her Henry, their cozy home, and the love that lived there.

Love. That was at the crux of the entire matter for Hannah. *Lack* of love, actually. Even as a child, Gussie had recognized the sad lack in Hannah's life. And she had seen the efforts Hannah had made to be approved, to be loved. And she had recognized when finally Hannah had settled for an acceptance of her own unlovableness. Unlovable and unlovely—that was Hannah's opinion of herself.

Saddest of all, perhaps, was the way Hannah had equated her earthly father's lack of love with her Heavenly Father's. Gussie remembered clearly the Sunday School hour when the leader asked for favorite hymn selections. Pansy could be counted on to suggest "Jesus Loves Me." With gusto, if not with harmony, the children had sung with shining faces. All but Hannah.

"How do you *know* He loves you?" she had argued. "You shouldn't lie, you know. P'raps He doesn't."

"Hannah! How can you say that?" Gussie had asked, scandalized, and quoted from the song itself, "The Bible tells me so."

"That's a *song*," Hannah sniffed. "How do you *know*?"

"I don't know, 'xacly," Gussie had confessed. "But I know He does!"

Mrs. Loy, swiftly interrupting the whispered argument among her pupils, had said, "Hannah, dear, you pick one you like," and had looked taken aback at the request.

"At the Cross," Hannah had said, and after a flurry to locate the unchildish hymn, the children had struggled through one verse:

> *Alas! and did my Savior bleed?*
> *And did my Sov'reign die?*
> *Would He devote that sacred head*
> *For such a worm as I?*

Hannah sang with gusto. Gussie knew now, of course, that the reassurance of the chorus was beyond the ability of children to understand, and they were left with the sound of Hannah's trebled "Was it for crimes that I have done / He groaned upon the tree?" ringing hollowly in their hearts.

Had Mrs. Loy attempted to explain and to emphasize the hymn's eventual summation, "And now I am happy all the day!"? Gussie supposed she had, but at the time she and Pansy were too shocked at their friend's audacity in questioning their basic childish concept, that God loved them, to hear what the teacher may have said.

Later, crawling into her father's lap, Gussie had tried to talk about it.

"Hannah—Hannah said how do I know God loves me?"

"And do you know?" her father had asked.

"I *know* He does," Gussie answered stoutly, twining her small arms around her father's neck and holding him tightly to her.

It was then her father had taught her John 3:16: "For God so loved the world that he gave his only begotten Son, that whosoever believeth in him should not perish, but have everlasting life."

Twenty years later and separated from her father by hundreds of miles, Gussie never doubted his love. And consequently, she relied as supremely on her Heavenly Father's love for her.

Hannah, across the years, had to all appearances conformed in spiritual matters, as in all else. She had been faithful in church attendance, had learned the catechism, had submitted to baptism, and had joined the neighborhood church. She knelt at proper times, sang in unison, gave her offerings and later her tithes, eventually served on committees, and now—faced the distinct possibility of becoming a pastor's wife. And all, Gussie thought sadly, without a loving relationship with her Heavenly Father.

It seemed natural to talk about one friend with another. "I'm waiting for an answer from Hannah," she said now to Dovie, for of course Dovie knew about Gussie's little scheme to match Hannah with Matthew Hunter. Knew and approved. Her own love affair, having come late in life, continually filled her formerly starved heart with wonder.

"Knowing what little I do about Hannah," Dovie said, "it seems a little risky to me. What if Matthew, after all, rejects the idea—or, heaven forbid, waits until she might come, in response to his proposal, and then see her and refuse to go through with it."

"You make it sound as if Hannah is—well, uncomely. She's not! She's a perfectly ordinary-looking person, which is what I would consider myself—nothing particularly beautiful, perhaps, but certainly nothing—uncomely. The trouble with Hannah is that she *thinks* she's—uncomely." Gussie seemed to be having trouble describing her "ordinary" friend. "The trouble is," she repeated, "she's convinced she's plain, and that it matters to people."

"Matthew, of course, is one gorgeous man," Dovie said, adding, "or *was.* He's had his pick of the available charmers. Or *did*—"

"That's what makes it so perfect, Dovie! Matthew thinks women have fallen for him just because he was such a catch. He's truly quite bitter about the fact that his disfigurement has changed their opinion of him. Hannah is fixated on the idea that no man will love her for herself. And I must admit that having all that money hasn't helped. Now she's suspicious of every male glance. Except for Delbert Bly—"

"The minister."

"And a truly good man. But too old and too settled in his bachelorhood since the death of his wife. And too—too *prosaic* for Hannah. Hannah, whether she knows it or not, has poetry in her soul. She would love the bush," Gussie said earnestly. "Oh, I hope she writes soon!"

With Hanky seated on a chair at the side of the table with a cookie and a glass of milk, the two friends chatted amiably over their tea. Finally Gussie rose, helped wash the lettuce for Dovie's supper preparations, and took her departure.

"Be sure and let me know when something happens," she urged, as she always did.

"You know Anna will come and everything will be all right," Dovie answered with a smile, as she always did in the face of her friend's concern.

"I'm available," Gussie insisted, as *she* always did. Both reassured, they parted, Dovie to her rocker and another upward request to "Suffer the little children to come unto me," Gussie to her home and the letter that had been dropped off by a neighbor returning from the post office at Meridian.

"Tell Matthew to write," she read, her heart swelling with joy.

"Oh, Hannah, I will, I will! And now, Matthew Hunter, it's up to you! I know," she spoke feelingly to the absent Matthew, "you won't hurt my Hannah."

8

DA . . . WHERE'S MY DA?"

Shading her eyes against the blazing sun, Holly stared up into the grave face of a total stranger.

The squinted eyes in the weathered face were full of compassion.

"He's—your daddy—that is, he's back there." And the man's head tipped in the direction of the back of the wagon. "But maybe you shouldn't—"

But Holly was lifting aside her skirt, stepping onto the hub of the rear wheel, and pulling herself up. At sight of the horror that touched that small face, the driver groaned and muttered, "*Said* I didn't want to be the one to bring him back!"

In the wagon bed, among the wood he had gathered for his fire, the groceries he had bought, and the sloshing barrels he had filled, lay the crumpled form of Edward Carroll. Crumpled in a pool of blood, his face white, his eyes closed.

"Da! Da—speak to me!" As Holly, wild-eyed, prepared to scramble over the side of the wagon, the man on the wagon seat spoke.

"He ain't dead, girlie. But," he muttered under his breath, "he sure-enough soon *will* be.

"Wait a minute, girlie. You cain't help any thataway. Go fix a bed—in the shade if you can, and I'll get him down."

"What's wrong?" the child cried. "What's happened to my Da?"

"I don't rightly know," the man said, making his way laboriously down off the high seat. "I was at the coulee when he stopped for wood and water. When he was a-loading the barrels, he just sorta gasped and grabbed his chest."

"The blood—"

"Oh, that ain't serious, I'd say. When he fell he banged his head something terrible on the tailgate. It's swoll up some and looks bad, but it's that other thing—that trouble in his chest—what's serious, I'd say."

As he talked, the man had removed the tailgate and began the process of unloading.

"Sissy—what's the matter?" Neddy, wakened by the racket, had come sleepily to look up at his sister as she continued staring into the wagon.

"It's Da, Neddy—he's hurt."

"Here, boy," the man said, not unkindly, handing Neddy a bundle of wood. The child staggered with it toward the campfire area, dropped it, and returned to stand, staring up at his sister's pale face.

"Come, girlie," the man said, "get down and help. I'll hand you and the little feller what you can handle, and we'll have your Da out of here in jig time."

The man had untied his own horse, which had been tied to the back of the wagon, and soon the contents were removed. Though burly, the man grunted under the load of the barrels, muttering, "Be jest my luck to have a heart spasm too." Nevertheless, he set the barrels in the shade of the dugout, lifted out the groceries, and then, reaching into the wagon, grasped Edward's foot and pulled the unconscious man toward him. With another grunt he heaved the limp form onto his shoulder and carried it to the dugout. Holly had preceded him and had spread blankets and a pillow.

Edward Carroll's body slid to the ground, and the man and Holly straightened the limbs as one would straighten a rag doll.

Dipping a kettle into the water barrel, Holly brought it to the side of her father, located a towel, and began sponging the colorless face and injured head.

The man watched for a few minutes. Then, looking around, seeing little else to do, he said, "I feel awful bad to do this, girlie, but I gotta go. I got a wagon and another horse back there at the coulee. Jest so happened your da and I got to talkin', and he told me whereabouts his claim was—that's how come I could bring him home."

Holly's shaking fingers were mopping at the cut that slowly continued to ooze blood. Neddy, face as white as that of the injured man, stood helplessly by.

"I hafta go now, girlie—"

"Yes. Yes I know. What'll I do, Mister?"

The child's eyes, enormous in her stricken face, caused the man to move uneasily and to promise, "I'll send some-one—you can count on that. I'll get my wagon and things and go on to the town. By night, I think, someone will come."

Helplessly, the man patted the shoulder of the girl—child—and turned to his waiting horse.

Only when she heard the dim sounds of the horse's hooves did Holly, with a start, raise her head, look toward the retreating man, and cry, "Neddy, run after him and thank him! Mama would want us to do that."

Without a word, Neddy ran out onto the prairie and lifted his little-boy voice to call into the vast spaces the words his mama, and now his sister, knew to be proper: "Thanks, Mister!"

If the stranger's eyes misted and his heart smote him, no one ever knew. Any sound was lost in the prairie's vacuum of silence. Any tear was dried by its remorseless wind.

When Neddy crawled into the strip of shade to huddle at his sister's side, Holly was still doggedly applying wet cloths to her father's face.

"Is Da dead—too?" the boy asked anxiously, his memory still filled with the loss of his mother.

"No—no, Neddy. He's just—asleep. He'll wake up—you'll see."

The day waned, and the sun—wearying of its relentless course—dropped toward the western horizon. And still the man "slept."

"You sit here, Neddy, and hold the cloth on his forehead," Holly said finally, noting her brother's lost look. "I think we better eat something."

Only then did she go through the box of supplies. "Tell you what—we'll eat crackers and cheese. In the morning I'll get the fire going and make some pancakes."

"Soup, Sissy?"

Lifting up a foul-smelling, newspaper-wrapped, bloody lump, Holly blanched. The meat, faithfully obtained by her father as promised, had quickly spoiled.

"I'll make you some soup tomorrow, Neddy," she promised. "If I can open the cans." And Holly looked doubtfully at the tins and her own small hands.

"We better bury this, Neddy." Wise beyond her years, the girl refrained from expressing her fears that the spoiled meat might attract some wild animal—perhaps coyotes, whose distant cries often sent her shivering in the night to sleep beside her da.

Their father's spade was nearby, and the ground was easier to dig where Edward Carroll had been cutting the squared pieces of sod for the walls and roof of his dugout. Together they buried the noxious package and piled the soil over it, mounding it bit by bit until it resembled a miniature grave, not unlike many they had seen along the trail on their arduous trek. Holly had never been able to forget some of the crudely lettered headstones: "Here lies

Clara's boy, his mother's pride, his father's joy." "Three days he blest us, then he left us." "Sleep now and rest, we journey ever west."

When they returned to the shadow of the dugout, Edward had not stirred. Freshening the towel and laying it on his brow, Holly turned to the supplies: Uncle Jerry's pancake flour; oatmeal, C grade, coarse cut; rolled wheat "partly cooked, very desirable"; a bag of marrowfat peas; beans—red kidney and genuine Swedish brown; a one-pound package of granula (forms one of the best-known foods for infants and children) "This is thrice cooked and will keep for years." Da had chosen well.

The prairie store had offered a good choice of canned goods. Neddy should have his soup: puree of white beans; mulligatawny; oxtail; puree of green peas; tomato . . .

One worry—that of what they should eat—was lifted from the thin shoulders. But how to get into the cans? Right now Holly wanted to open condensed milk. Added to a cup of water, it would be nourishing for Neddy's small bones.

Holly studied the can opener, grasping the oak handle properly, but hesitating before making the slashing motion that would penetrate the metal. If she should miss! Her bent knee was uncomfortably close as she knelt amid the piled goods.

"Bring me Da's hammer," she commanded a watching (and thirsty) Neddy.

With it in her right hand and the steel blade of the can opener firmly positioned by her left hand, Holly struck a blow.

"You did it, Sissy!" Neddy held out a cup of water.

"Wait, Neddy. I have to do it again. It needs two holes, for some reason."

The second blow was a little lopsided and the can tipped. Quickly Holly righted it, with only a few drops spilled. Neddy's water was liberally laced with condensed milk and greedily drunk. He filled the cup with water again, and again Holly poured the milk, this time drinking thirstily herself.

"I wish I could get some of it down Da," Holly fretted. But when she tipped a spoonful into her father's slack mouth, it ran out.

The children sat mournfully at the side of the man while the long evening shadows crept over the rim of the world.

"Is he dead, Sissy?" Neddy asked.

"No, Neddy. See—here in his neck you can see a little fluttery thing, if you watch caref'ly."

The children watched the slight throb, the only sign of life aside from the faint move of the chest. Neddy's eyes drooped, and Holly laid him down and covered him against the evening's slightly cooler air.

Hour by hour she sat at the side of her father, bending to catch a sound of the erratic heartbeat, moistening the towel, and trying to still the panic that swelled in her own small bosom.

Finally, worn out past enduring, her head drooped, her thin body slumped, and Holly, in spite of herself, slept.

Slept and dreamed. Dreamed of roses, wild and sweet and abundant. And among them Rose, her mother, gathering a bouquet. Gathering them, holding them out to her daughter, and smiling. Smiling and whispering, "Wildrose, Sissy . . ."

Slept and dreamed. Dreamed of voices—soft, sympathetic, whispering: "Poor little things! Whatever will become of them . . . don't wake them yet . . . help me . . . move him . . ."

Slept, dreamed, and woke. Woke to a nightmare.

Holly's cry rent the early morning stillness: "Da! Da! Where is my da?"

9

NEEDING REST AND PEACE FOR A CERTAIN AGITA-
tion of her spirit—the result of her seemingly rash response to Gussie's letter—Hannah, to her annoyance,
found the Sunday morning service to be anything but
helpful.

It didn't look encouraging when the first hymn was
"More Secure Is No One Ever." Although she loved the old
Swedish melody, the words, having become familiar across
the years, never failed to distress her. It began innocently
enough:

> *More secure is no one ever*
> *Than the loved ones of the Savior—*
> *Not yon star on high abiding*
> *Nor the bird in home-nest hiding.*

So far so good. Believing (with her head if not her
heart) that Jesus loved the world was reasonable.

True, there had been a time in childhood when she had
argued the point, prompted by Gussie's and Pansy's hearty
singing of "Jesus Loves Me." Subsequent arguments, talks,
Bible readings, and sermons had convinced Hannah that Jesus indeed must have had great love to die for the sins of
the world. (The world—but Hannah personally?)

And the Father? Hannah's voice faltered and was finally no more than a moving of the lips as the hymn proceeded:

God His own doth tend and nourish,
In His holy courts they flourish;
Like a father kind He spares them,
In His loving arms He bears them.

Nice words. But to Hannah—only words. Borne in a father's arms? She had no memory of it, and her barren heart testified of it.

What He takes or what He gives us
Shows the Father's love so precious;
We may trust His purpose wholly—
'Tis His children's welfare solely.

There were times, still, when Hannah's heart cried out for her father's love. Too late—too late. There were times, like now, when her heart cried out, even anguished, for the knowledge of a Heavenly Father's love. Rather, hearing and mouthing the words of hymn selection number two, "Day by Day," she struggled with bitterness.

Day by day and with each passing moment,
    Strength I find to meet my trials here.
Trusting in my Father's wise bestowment,
    I've no cause for worry or for fear.
He whose heart is kind beyond all measure
    ["Words—words!"]
    Gives unto each day what He deems best—
Lovingly ["lovingly?"], *its part of pain and pleasure,*
    Mingling toil with peace and rest.

Hymns and sermons were to be coordinated, it seemed. Delbert, with his usual thoroughness, took as his text 1 John 4:16 and read it with full effect: "God is love; and he that dwelleth in love dwelleth in God, and God in him."

Lost in the bleakness of her response, Hannah tuned out the sermon.

Rich in worldly possessions, with nothing she wanted beyond her means, living in plenty, even in luxury, Hannah was poor. Unable to "dwell" in love, she was denied the presence and assurance not only of a loving God but of others. Unworthy—unworthy.

Could she hope to have a successful marriage? What she had to offer—it might be enough for Delbert Bly. But would it be enough for—for any man not caught up in other-worldly matters? A man like Matthew Hunter? For Hannah had not misunderstood Gussie's letter: Matthew Hunter, while not as blatantly seeking a wife as many who advertised for them, was not going to play games. His response—if he wrote—and hers would set the tone of their future relationship.

Thankfully, Hannah thought now, she was not a silly, simpering female, full of impossible dreams and romantic expectations. She was, after all, a businesswoman. And this relationship, she could see, was an affair of business. Both partners would make an investment—time, patience, kindness, work (especially work)—and the dividends would be satisfaction in a job well done, fulfillment in establishing a homestead in the bush, and—perhaps—the joy of raising a family.

Yes, a business arrangement between two sensible people could hold great possibilities. But was it enough? Apparently it was for Matthew Hunter; it would be for her. In fact, what a relief it would be not to have to live up to anyone's expectations! Just to be herself—that would be the bargain.

But "herself"—without her money—would it be enough? In spite of herself, Hannah shivered. Stiffening her shoulders, she realized that she had come thus far without love; she could make it the rest of the way.

But why hadn't Delbert's passionless companionship been enough? Hannah stirred uneasily and quickly closed the door on the thought.

And—if it worked out—she would be near her beloved Gussie. Gussie and Pansy had given her the only unearned love she had known. Thank God for them!

Yes, thank God. She might not be able to thank Him for His love (though she tried, desperately and hopelessly, at times), but she could thank Him wholeheartedly for Gussie and Pansy.

So it was with an honest heart she stood with the others for the Doxology and sang, "Praise God, from whom all blessings flow."

And would those blessings, given so undeservedly, include at long last a husband and a home in a distant, beckoning place called Wildrose?

 **10**

SLOWLY THE WORLD CAME INTO FOCUS; THE sleepy eyes jolted from dreams to reality.

Already the sun threatened its continued heat; the breeze whispered of sweltering hours to follow.

Inside the dugout Neddy slept, his face rosy and sweet, if slightly grimy. Beyond the circle of shade human forms moved uneasily, dark against the brightness of the rising sun and looming over the prone figures of the children.

Half taking it all in, Holly awoke to reach automatically toward the nearby blanket—to find it gone. Gone, too, the quiet form it had covered.

"Da! What have you done with my da?"

The looming figures became flesh and blood, murmuring words of sympathy and explanation. Shadows became hands, reaching helpless promises toward the frantic child.

"Where is he? Where is he?"

"Now, now," a soothing voice said, its comfort swallowed by the child's shrieks.

Rising, staggering, evading the arms stretched toward her, Holly tumbled from the dugout to glance wildly around the camping site.

As though drawn by a magnet, she turned stumbling feet in the direction of a nearby wagon. Finding it empty, she climbed the side of a second. There, as on the preceding afternoon, she found the figure of her father, this time recognized by his boots, the rest of him swathed in the familiar blanket.

In a tremble to get the smothering weight off his face, Holly tumbled into the rig—

Eventually the reaching hands, sympathetic voices, and concerned strangers lifted the limp, sobbing creature from the wagon and returned her to the comparative shade of the dugout. Shudder after shudder wracked the thin frame.

Only when Neddy touched her, crying piteously, "Sissy! Sissy—what's wrong?" did she reach beyond herself to her brother and think of something other than the cold, set face in the wagon bed.

Neddy, already well familiar with death and separation, understood the hiccuped words. Finally, silent and still he lay, safe in his sister's arms.

But safe only briefly. Other hands, firm hands, lifted him from her—lifted her, limp and yielding, from him.

"Sissy! Sissy! Sissy!" Now it was the boy's turn to shriek, reaching over the shoulder of the man who carried him, frantically trying to return to the only security left to him on the face of the vast world.

"It's worse than I thought . . . ," muttered one grim voice.

"Poor babies . . ."

"What's to become of them . . . ?"

"You take the boy in your rig—I'll take the girl . . ."

This set up such a fury of twisting and fighting and screaming and hitting on Neddy's part that the scheme was abandoned for the sake of peace.

In his sister's arms again, Neddy and Holly crouched in the bottom of a wagon, while around them voices and movement indicated that their family's possessions were being loaded and divided until, it seemed, every trace of the Carrolls and their temporary stay was erased.

All but the half-finished dugout. As the wagons started off with a jerk, through the open tailgate Holly cast a despairing glance back: stark, empty, already suffering the ravages of the rising wind, the dugout alone held for a brief time its small cache of memories: sounds of weeping, moments of hope, hours of hopelessness; its smell of sweat, its footprints already disappearing before the wind, its blackened fire sifting its ashes into the prairie soil, and its dreams and nightmares dissipated with the smoke.

And at its side—symbol of hope, proof of hopelessness—a brave pink flower opened its fragrance to the day.

Holly's eyes, dry now and for a long time to come, saw the small rose as a beacon. It was the last thing she saw as the wagons tipped the edge of the world and rolled across the plains toward town.

Toward town and the cemetery. First there was a stop at the undertaker's. The small band of neighbors waited and talked as the body of Edward Carroll was prepared for burial. There could be no delay—the heat was oppressive. And no, the child had said, there were no relatives to be informed. There was no place to go . . .

"Here we go again," one man said sadly. "Hasn't been too long since the Doernbeck tragedy. Those children are with you, ain't they, Waggoner?"

"Yes, and I can't rightly take no more."

"We know that. Let's see—the Wayburns, maybe—"

"Naw. She's bedfast most of the time—a baby every year, and all of them sickly."

"Jake . . . you and Adeline . . . ?"

"Can't," Jake said firmly. "Last thing Addie said to me—we can't take them in, Jake, and I knew 'twas the truth."

"Whipple?"

Alarmed, Whipple hedged. "My sister ain't here to ask—"

"You ain't got any kids, either of you. Couldn't you use a little help on that place of yours?"

"Sure, but look at the boy—just a baby. And the girl—

skinny as a rat." Moses Whipple looked a little shamefaced but determined.

"Crabbe? How about you and Elsie?"

Sylvester Crabbe looked alarmed.

"Somebody's got to take 'em, Syl! For heaven's sake, man, have some pity!"

"Say—I don't know about such a responsibility—"

"Well, go talk to Elsie about it. What's more, you would take all the belongings—tools, cookware, wagon, and such. Even the horses. That OK with the rest of you?"

Everyone nodded agreeably.

"There was enough cash in his pocket—from his buffalo bone money, I guess—to pay for the funeral."

Holly and Neddy, crouched in the shade of the funeral parlor, listened and watched. Neddy couldn't take it all in; Holly was numb with shock and unbelief. How could strangers decide their future? But what choice did they have? Despair, like a lump of prairie sod, settled into her middle, and its legacy was a sudden retching.

"Poor little tykes!"

"Haven't eaten, after all—"

"Get some water—"

Kind hands, strange hands, did their awkward best. Watching women pointed out the pitiful scene to Elsie Crabbe, stirring her sympathy, calling to mind her Christian duty, pointing out the advantages of a ready-made family . . . the joys of parenthood . . .

"I guess I know my Christian duty," she said stiffly. "We'll do our best."

Concerned townsfolk and outlying farmers and their wives looked relieved. Now many a voice was raised: "Sure wish I coulda done it," "My turn next," and "God bless you for your Christian charity!"

Numb, unbelieving, and sick of body, Holly climbed with help into the Crabbe wagon, turning always to assist Neddy. There on the rumbling ride to the small cemetery

Neddy slept, to be roused at last to stand at his sister's side and watch as another coffin was lowered into the ground and another mound heaped and abandoned. Someone said a few words; someone prayed. Someone laid a few prairie flowers on the grave.

Someone—Elsie Crabbe—took two small hands in hers and herded the hollow-eyed children toward a wagon. Down numerous roads and trails the homesteaders wended their way back to soddy or dugout, newly erected frame house or shack, knowing it could be their turn next—to end it all in tragedy or to rally to the support of an indigent family. And few if any among them would have loosed their grip on the opportunity to own land of their own or would have forsaken confidence that they would yet see this threatening—and challenging—land blossom as the rose.

✻ ✻ ✻

"Here we are—home."

The words roused Holly from her half-sleep. Rising to her feet stiffly from her bed in the bottom of the wagon, she shook Neddy gently.

"Wake up, Neddy."

"Where are we?"

"Home," the woman said.

"We'll be here—for a while," Holly said.

"Home" was a bleak frame house, but no bleaker than most others. It was the absence of trees—or anything, for that matter—on the horizon. Holly had grown accustomed to the endless, empty vistas, but she had never liked it. Now it seemed lonelier, more intimidating than ever.

Standing in the wagon, she lifted her eyes and looked all around. Nothing but grass.

"Where are the hills?" she asked.

"Hills?" Elsie Crabbe asked blankly.

"Which direction are they—the trees, the bush, I mean."

"Over there, about 20 miles." Mrs. Crabbe pointed north.

"Do you go there for wood?"

"Yes, every once in awhile."

Still Holly stared into the emptiness that was north.

"Come, dear," Mrs. Crabbe said finally. "There'll be plenty of times you'll stare off into space." And grimness colored the words with certainty.

"Here—each of you take some of this stuff." Mrs. Crabbe pointed to the tumbled pile of the Carrolls' belongings. Holly picked up her mother's small Bible, brushed it off lovingly, and clutched it to her thin frame. Mrs. Crabbe thrust a bundle of clothes into Neddy's arms.

Sylvester Crabbe lifted the children to the ground, helped set out the remaining possessions, and turned toward the barn; it, unlike the house, was of sod. A few chickens scrabbled in an enclosed pen; a cow was tethered beyond the barn, its face in the abundant grasses. At least there would be milk for Neddy.

The narrow house—two rooms down, two up—was blazingly hot. Elsie Crabbe threw open the door and windows to catch any errant breeze and began stowing the accumulation of Carroll effects on shelves, on nails, and in corners.

"We'll have to wash most of this," she said, with a sniff, holding up Da's grubby work pants. "Too long in the leg for Syl. But," she cast a critical eye on Neddy, "they'll cut down to make a couple of pairs for you." She sighed.

Holly looked around at the strange place—walls thinly calcimined; bare floor; a worn plush couch, its tassels limp; a few chairs; the regulation air-tight heater; and on the wall a large, ornately framed painting of a huge dog. A Saint Bernard, Holly thought, lying on what seemed to be a sort of pier. Sprawled across the dog's massive front legs lay a small boy in such a way as to make the viewer believe he had just been pulled from the dashing waves below.

Neddy stared, fascinated. "Is he dead, Sissy?" he whispered.

But not too softly not to be heard by Elsie Crabbe. "That's the special thing about that picture," she said, pausing in her task of sorting laundry—white pile, colored pile, dark pile. "Everybody interprets it for himself. Now, I personally believe the child is dead—"

"He's not!" Holly spoke quickly. "He's resting, Neddy." And she put her arm around the small boy, who had shrunk against her at the woman's words.

"Hoity-toity!" Elsie Crabbe said, studying the thin, defiant figure of the girl and the dismal face of the boy. "Well, never mind. That's another thing you'll have plenty of time to study. There's not much else—"

Holly's eyes fixed on a small bookshelf and its contents: A Bible, the ubiquitous catalog, some tattered copies of *The Youth's Companion,* and a few books. The titles, what she could make out, included *Medical Companion and Household Physician* and—joy of joys—several volumes of the works of J. Fenimore Cooper: *The Deerslayer, The Pathfinder, The Prairie, The Pioneers.*

"Can I read those?" she asked, her eyes alight.

"Of course, my dear—unless," dubiously, "they are too old for you."

"They're not!" and again the light of battle was in the dark eyes. "I've already read *The Last of the Mohicans,* and there, in my mother's things, you'll find *Gulliver's Travels* and *Last Days of Pompeii*—"

"Hoity-toity!" Elsie Crabbe said again, and Holly subsided.

"Here, dear," Elsie continued calmly. "Take these things up to the room on the left," and she pointed to a stack of Neddy's clothes. "When you come down, you can help me get supper ready. It's been a long day without decent meals."

The "decent meal" consisted of boiled potatoes, bacon,

turnips and—Holly's mouth watered—bread and butter. There was milk for both children.

While Holly and Mrs. Crabbe did the dishes and continued tidying the house, Neddy sat solemnly on the couch, his cheeks flushed, his eyes heavy.

"I don't think Neddy feels too good," Holly said anxiously.

"Neddy—what kind of a name is that?" the woman asked, soaping a kettle.

"It's for my father. His name is—was—Edward."

"I should think Eddie would be more fitting."

"Mama called him Neddy," Holly said stubbornly and listened for a "Hoity-toity."

Mrs. Crabbe sighed, dried her hands, went over to the couch, and felt the little boy's forehead. Her gaunt face took on a look of concern.

"There's some fever there. Stick out your tongue, young Edward."

Neddy obediently put out his tongue, and it was duly studied.

"Has he had the measles?" Never having had children of her own, the middle-aged woman was at a loss.

"Maybe a bath," Holly suggested, "a cool bath. That's what Mama always did when he got feverish."

"Needs to get all that grime off too—that's for certain. I'll get the tub ready; you get him ready."

"What's up?" Sylvester came in, setting a pail of milk on the table in the kitchen where Elsie was busy dipping water from the reservoir on the range.

"The young one—he seems to be sick. I didn't count on that, Syl!" Elsie sighed heavily, clearly burdened by her Christian duty.

"Only natural," Syl responded cheerfully. "Been through a lot today, those two."

Holly put Neddy, ominously quiet about it all, into the tub and bathed the small body, washed the red-gold curls, and then dried him well and put him in one of her father's shirts.

"You too," Elsie said. "Water's precious. And you need it!"

Closing the door after she settled Neddy on the couch with a well-thumbed catalog in his lap, Holly stripped her dusty clothes from her weary body, slid into the tepid water, and scrubbed herself "all over" for the first time in weeks. If a few tears mingled with the few dippersful of water allowed for the rite, who could tell?

Holly was back in her clothes and struggling to drag the tub outside when Elsie burst in.

"Wait!" she shrieked. "Water's precious!"

Much taken aback, Holly stammered, "I know that—I wasn't going to dump it."

Fanning her heated face, Elsie Crabbe urged Holly to take young Edward and go on upstairs. "I've been fixin' beds, and I'll be right up."

In the room "on the left," a simple, paint-chipped iron bed stood invitingly turned down. As well as a small dresser and commode, the room held what Elsie Crabbe called a shakedown, obviously an improvised sleeping accommodation.

"Now then, young Edward, into bed!" And the woman directed Neddy toward the pallet on the floor. "And you, Miss, into the bed."

"Neddy can sleep with me," Holly said.

Mrs. Crabbe looked shocked. "Certainly not!"

"He does, sometimes," Holly explained, "like when he's sick or when he's afraid—like now."

An ugly red stained the woman's face. "Surely you know better than that—a big girl like you!"

Holly's straight, dark brows drew together over her eyes in puzzlement.

"My mama—"

"Your mama! Your mama isn't here, and if she were,

I'd tell her the same thing: It ain't right and proper for him to sleep with you."

"My mama told me to look after my brother—".

"You can look after him well enough with him here— you there. We'll have to do something else eventually—put him on the couch, maybe—"

"No! Leave him here. He'll—he'll be fine." And Holly turned toward the bed and the clean gown Mrs. Crabbe had found for her.

"Well, good night then. Don't forget to say your prayers."

Only a little light of the long evening remained when Holly slipped into bed. But she could see the apprehension in the big eyes looking at her over the edge of the blanket. Holly held out her arms.

Cuddling the hot body to her, soothing the limbs that jerked from time to time as the tired, frightened, sick little boy drifted off to a feverish sleep, Holly sang softly.

"Nonee-no, nonee-no, nonee-no, nonee-no . . ."

11

PANSY WAS WAITING PATIENTLY OUTSIDE THE door of Vaughn's Royal Emporium, critically studying an elegantly displayed set of Electric Gold Glassware. Against its draping of dark blue velvetta, the "Newest Things in Fancy Glassware" reflected the strategically placed lights for an eye-catching effect. Indeed, "none but an expert can tell it is not genuine cut glass." Certainly not Pansy, to whom it looked like the real thing.

"So honest," she thought, loyally. "But that's Hannah! Her father, now, would have let it pass—to the ignorant, like me—for the genuine thing. And would have asked a handsome price for it too!" Hannah's reliability in this, as in all else, paid off. Her clientele trusted her word and her wares.

Genuine or imitation, it was beautiful, and Pansy sighed enviously. Buell's small salary at the newspaper would never allow for such extravagances: The Electric Gold Berry Set, with its bowl and six saucers for $2.90, could, for $1.75, add an additional six saucers. The Electric Gold Lemonade Set consisted of one jug, six tumblers, and one nickel tray; and the Electric Gold Four Piece Set, without which the full effect would be lacking, consisted of cream pitcher, butter dish, sugar bowl, and spoon holder.

"I could start without the lemonade set," Pansy mused, "what with lemons unavailable most of the year and terribly expensive when they are. Oh, there you are,

Hannah! Are you going to take an Electric Gold Set to the bush?" Pansy's laughing tone was her own answer.

"Teaser! You don't even know whether or not I'm going! And if I do, you can be sure an Electric Gold Set is the last thing I'll take. In fact, I'll take very little."

Hannah, to her own amazement, was talking as if she really were going. But her mind had been filled with little else since receiving Gussie's astonishing letter. Although there was a core of quivering doubt somewhere deep inside, with a surprisingly steely determination she had already made the decision to take the step that would, irrevocably and forever, change her life's direction.

Her last association with Delbert Bly had laid to rest the final hesitation. Dinner Friday night (at her house, of course, and, of course, properly and circumspectly overseen by Hannah's house-help, Tilda and Malachi), over dessert she had, rather cleverly, she thought, introduced the slumbering subject of marriage.

"Well, Delbert," she had offered lightly, banteringly, "did the hosiery purchase turn out to your satisfaction?"

Delbert carefully dabbed his lips with his serviette, brightened, and responded. "Excellently, thank you! What a superior quality of goods Vaughn's offers after all."

"I trust you—ah—," Hannah had the grace to blush a little as she wove her devious web, "—discarded those you mentioned were worn through."

"Indeed," Delbert said, deflated by the unhappy thought. "Or," he added honestly, "I soon will. There is, after all—" His tone turned thoughtful.

"Yes, Delbert? Proceed."

"There is, after all, little hope of their being darned. Mrs. Smithers [the lady who "did" for him] will never condescend to add darning to her already overburdened household chores."

"And they are too worn to be put into the missionary barrel?"

"Now," Delbert brightened again, "that is an idea. Thank you, my dear! What an idea! . . ."

Delbert, as always, faltered.

"Minister's wife I would make," Hannah finished for him gently.

Delbert looked distinctly uncomfortable, as always when the subject got this far.

"I could think of none better," Delbert finished gallantly, if lamely.

Silence reigned as Delbert cleaned out his tapioca sauce dish, added sugar to his coffee, stirred it, and sipped—one, two, three times.

"Delbert," Hannah said, finally, "you still harbor warm feelings for your late wife."

"Oh, Hannah, you do understand!" Delbert grasped the thought with more passion than he had ever allowed himself previously.

"And may continue to do so—"

"Ah, possibly. One has to be cautious about these, ah, enduring situations." And again, as previously, Hannah suspicioned that Delbert never had fit into double harness as appreciatively as he might have.

The truth was, Delbert was perfectly happy in his single state. With Mrs. Smithers to cook and wash for him and a deaconess to care for the flowers, all he really needed— Hannah found herself threatened with hysteria—was someone to darn his socks!

To think that her life, her future, hung by a slender strand of darning wool! To darn or not to darn: that is the question—Hannah found herself almost dizzy with relief and giddy with release.

How remarkable then that she had picked up her coffee cup with perfectly controlled fingers, had sipped with absolute decorum, had taken a last spoonful of tapioca as if her very world had not spun and settled into a new orbit!

Eventually, helping Delbert into his coat and handing

him his gloves, Hannah said simply and straightforwardly, "I think it might be a good idea, Delbert, if you found someone else to do the flowers."

Delbert had stood transfixed for a moment. Then humbly, honestly, he had said, "I suppose you are right, my dear."

Hannah, of course, had shared with Pansy the letter from Gussie with its world-tipping idea. Though she was torn between the wonder of the plan and the pain of losing yet another friend, Pansy was ecstatic at the prospect offered Hannah.

"Just think! How romantic! Sort of like in olden days when marriages were arranged—still are in some parts of the world."

"Romance doesn't have a thing to do with it," Hannah cautioned firmly. "This is as businesslike as anything I've been doing in the store. I've added up the assets and debits and made my decision. And," she added thoughtfully, "however it turns out, I'll abide by it. Life can't offer me much less than I have now," she finished quietly.

To Pansy, skimping and saving to make ends meet, it almost seemed incomprehensible that Hannah counted her wealth so light a thing. And to give it over for a life of deprivation in the bush country!

Pansy defended her position, saying now, "Money might make all the difference in the world to a homesteader! Think of Gussie's letters—the hard times they're having, trying to make it through these first few years!"

"That's just the point, Pansy," Hannah said in a hard voice. "Either he takes me as I am—just plain me—or not at all. One cannot buy love! And I will not buy a proposal!"

Pansy subsided. "So, how are you going to arrange all this?" And her waved gesture took in the store, Vaughn House, and everything in it.

"I haven't talked to Karl. But I will, if Matthew writes

what Gussie seemed to think he would. Karl can manage very well; Peter, his son, wants to learn the ropes, and this will be his opportunity. As for the house—I'm quite sure Tilda and Malachi will stay on and keep it in good shape."

And Pansy, knowing Tilda and Malachi and their story, was sure they would. Malachi, a burned-out fur trader, had gladly turned from the decimated buffalo herd and quickly disappearing beaver supply to doing odd jobs for Morris Vaughn. At Morris's death, he had moved into Vaughn House to add his protection and care and, in midlife, had married Tilda, a widow. Together they ran Hannah's house and were, they declared, as happy as "bugs in a rug." They would undoubtedly carry on admirably.

At her corner Pansy turned aside reluctantly. Her mother had the care of her children for a few hours, and Pansy must hurry home.

"Let me know—when you hear!" she urged.

"You'll be the first to know," Hannah promised, adding to herself as her friend hurried off, *and except for Karl and Gretel, probably the only one.*

Letting herself into the entrance to Vaughn House with its massive stained-glass ornamented double doors, Hannah laid aside her cape and hat and gloves. On a rich mahogany table in the hall lay the day's mail. Ignoring the ornate mirror directly above it, her fingers, strangely atremble in spite of her outward calmness, searched for an unfamiliar postmark. And when she found it, she held it, with a gasp, against her shirtwaist and saw it vibrate with the pounding of her heart.

"Is that you, Miss Hannah?"

"And who else would it be?" Hannah managed with a smile, as she did every evening.

Tilda, face flushed from a peek into the oven, smiled from the dining room before returning to her supper preparations.

Upstairs, in her room, Hannah closed the door, seated herself, and stared at the envelope with its momentous possibilities encased in it. Then, with a deep breath, she tore it open.

Dear Miss Vaughn:

This letter will come as no surprise to you, having been preceded by one from your friend and mine, Gussie Chapman.

If Gussie took it on herself to introduce me, I beg of you to discount most of what she may have said. I would not want you to have a mistaken opinion of me or my situation here in Wildrose.

I am a homesteader, Miss Vaughn, but believe I have expectations. Though what I have to offer is simple, even perhaps poor, at this time, I dare promise that things will improve immeasurably as time goes by. This means, of course, hard work and some deprivation for me and my family, should I be so fortunate to acquire one. Anyone sharing such a life will be subject to hard times, loneliness occasionally, makeshift worldly goods (but a sturdy house), and, perhaps a less-than-perfect mate thrown in!

In trying to be honest, I may have destroyed any hope of success to my purpose in writing. I would not want to misrepresent my situation or my person. I could promise faithfulness, respect, kindness, and a chance for a good and happy future.

Is it enough, Miss Vaughn? I cannot blame you if the chance seems too great. If, however, you are as willing as I to join hopes and dreams and efforts, I ask that you consider my letter a proposal of marriage.

Most sincerely yours,
Matthew Hunter

12

SUNDAY IN WILDROSE REALLY BEGAN ON SATURday.

For most people, the trip to church was a long one. Wagons, buggies, horseback, on foot—whatever method was available—brought the good folk of the district to meet with one another, and, in most cases, with their God. Whatever the reason, it was worth the effort, whether because of the physical contact or the spiritual uplift.

Whether or not one believed and obeyed the other nine commandments, everyone recognized the blessed practicality of the one that states: "Six days shalt thou labor, and do all thy work; but the seventh day is the sabbath of the LORD thy God."

And so plow and harrow, cultivator and seeder, disc and rake, reaper and binder were silent. There was no scrape of saw, no thud of grub hoe, no screech of grindstone. No anvil rang, no lathe turned, no bellows wheezed. Scythes, manure forks, post spades leaned in quiet corners. Not a hog ring was squeezed; no ear of horse, cow, sheep, swine, or dog knew the bite of a tattoo ear marker. No potato bug was picked, unless absentmindedly by a farmer thoughtfully walking the rows of his garden.

If the stipulated day of rest was appreciated—an oasis in a weary week—even the most pious among them recognized the wisdom and mercy of their "loophole" for necessary tasks. For hadn't their Lord himself healed on the Sabbath, and didn't He say, "Which of you shall have an ass or an ox fallen into a pit, and will not straightway pull him out on the sabbath day?"

And so the cows were milked, the stock fed, emergencies attended to.

For the wife and mother, Sunday's rest was all the more important because of Saturday's bustle. Meals were prepared ahead of time; in the summer perishables were kept for Sunday dinner in the depths of the well. When the people came home sleepy, hot, and hungry, half the work was done. In winter dinner could be waiting in an oven, perhaps cooling, but cooked.

Countless heads had to be washed on Saturday, and bodies bathed. Tangled hair must be brutally combed, stubborn hair curled. Papa's pants were pressed, small dresses were starched within an inch of their lives and had their frills and puckers and smocking and sashes ironed smooth. The week's manure was cleaned from boots, scuffed shoes shined, fingernails gouged free of goodness-knew-what-all. Neglected memory verses were feverishly looked up and singsonged until everyone in the house could quote the required passage by heart, whether or not they needed to.

On Sunday morning at church time, many a mother sank into her seat exhausted. But proud. Looking down a row of shining heads, shining shoes, and shining eyes, her heart swelled, and she gained strength to do the whole thing over again . . . and again . . . and again.

With church over and Sunday dinner eaten, Gussie plucked an already-sleeping Hanky from his high chair and took him off to bed. Henry pulled off his boots, leaned back in his rocking chair, put his feet up, and turned to a stack of the illustrated weekly paper *The Youth's Companion*, deemed by the pious to be acceptable Sunday reading. Nevertheless, it was full of worldly tidbits; Henry, however, rarely had time for them during the week. Any free moments in the summer found him dropping off into a nap. Today he was searching through the papers, sent in a bundle from time to time by Gussie's mother, for the fifth chapter in the continuing story "On the Lone Mountain Route—Conscience Makes Cowards." The illustration showed a bonneted young girl sitting disconsolately at the side of a path through the woods, a walking cane at her side, with a horse and rider approaching in the distance; it was appropriately titled "Delia's Dismay."

If memory served him right, Delia, wet with dew and shivering from her exposure to the mountain night, had reached her grandmother's cabin at dawn. Rheumatism, "the common enemy of the mountaineers," had seized the brave girl, and Granny's simples could not relieve her suffering. Where would she find the strength to make it to Sneedville and the jail where Joe, her brother, was falsely incarcerated? The picture hinted that she might just possibly be able to procure a ride; for she was obviously struggling on in spite of every adversity.

Ah yes! Henry's quick eye picked up a telling paragraph:

"Jeems," said Delia, "I'll give you that there white pig if you-uns'll let me have that horse today."

The stubborn boy refused to do so!

A dominicker rooster, a squirrel, and finally a Noah's ark, the one souvenir of Delia's childhood, were added to her bid.

Still the rascal refused!

"Henry! Are you reading ahead?" Gussie's reproachful voice caused Henry to start guiltily. "You are, aren't you?"

"I'll read something else," Henry promised immediately, turning quickly from the tantalizing story. "But hurry it up, or I'm apt to fall asleep waiting for you."

Gussie continued doggedly, neither hurried nor challenged. After all, Matthew Hunter was dropping by later on, and like any caring wife, Gussie was determined that everything would be shipshape. He shouldn't have opportunity to suppose his single estate, no matter how neat a house he kept, could compare with what a wife could do for him! Gussie peeked anxiously at the sugar twists, covered with a dish towel and awaiting warming and serving later on with a fresh pot of tea.

Gussie would have preferred serving a pie made from the rhubarb flourishing in her garden. But wisdom said otherwise when she checked her sugar supply and her egg supply and realized her sale of the last would not cover the purchase price of the first for some time to come.

And so, when she had baked bread yesterday, she had used part of the dough and made Mum's sugar twists. With a fourth of the recipe she had rolled the dough into an oblong, cut it into strips, shaped the strips into an "upside-down U," and crossed the dough skillfully, alternating from left to right (which for her was more convenient than Mum's right to left). The twist, when completed, was fastened together with a hat pin or skewer or any other such sharp household item, allowed to rise, and then dropped in deep fat and fried to a golden brown.

How often Gussie had watched, mouth watering, as Mum had used her old black-handled fork to turn the twists, then to hold the twists aloft until the fat had dripped off! Gussie felt much satisfaction in doing likewise. And when the twists were rolled in enough of her precious store of white sugar to coat them, she felt she had a dish fit for a king. But would Matthew Hunter think so? Knowing Matthew and his kindness, Gussie thought he wouldn't complain.

"Say," Henry said, looking up, "I wonder if we should pass this information on to Liza Kinski. It's about 'Hypophosphite of Lime and Soda.' 'Consumption and all lung diseases in early stages prevented and cured,' it says. 'Absolutely cured!'"

Gussie looked impressed. "What will they come up with next? What a time to be alive!"

"And this assures you'll stay that way! It is a pure solution and will not disarrange the most delicate stomach."

"Liza Kinski has the most delicate stomach in the Territories, if I understand her correctly—exceeded only by her weak lungs."

"She could at least send for the circular." And Henry made note of the location of the fascinating ad to share with his neighbor.

"Brother Victor should read this," Henry said with a chuckle. "'A minister submitted an account of tithes to a blacksmith. "But I don't go to your church!" the blacksmith exclaimed.

"'"No, but the door of my church is always open!" the minister replied.

"'Next day,'" Henry went on, "'the blacksmith submitted an account for shoeing to the minister. "But my horses are not shod at your smithy!" the minister exclaimed.

"'"No," was the reply, "but the door of my smithy is always open."' Ha!"

Gussie was rinsing out her dishrag.

"Surely they jest!" Henry said jocularly, reading something else with equal enjoyment.

"Now what?"

"'The chimes of Normandy could not excel in sweetness and purity the tone of the NEW DEPARTURE BICYCLE BELLS.'" Henry read with skeptical tones. "I find that hard to believe, Gussie.

"But say—this advertisement for Pearline Soap makes me wish I could get it for you. 'The rub board is pretty good for developing muscle,' they say, 'but it can't be healthy to breathe that tainted, fetid steam, and you'd better get your exercise in ways that are pleasanter.' 'Pearline,' they claim, 'will do this disagreeable work easily, quickly, and safely.' What do you say to that?"

"I say I'd just as soon stick with my Fels Naptha. I can't say I've noticed any *fetid* steam. Smelly, maybe, but not, ah, fetid."

Henry, no more sure of the word than his wife, couldn't argue the point.

"There is one race, Gussie," Henry said now, "apparently not cursed with dyspepsia. 'The sturdy little Eskimo . . . does not suffer from indigestion. The teeth of an Eskimo child will meet in a bit of walrus skin as the teeth of an American child would meet in the flesh of an apple.' And that, Gussie, when the hide of the walrus is from half an inch to an inch in thickness and bears considerable resemblance to the skin of an elephant. The Eskimo child will bite it, and digest it too, this article reports—and never know what dyspepsia means."

"Well, that's because he never hears the word," Gussie said reasonably. "He probably calls it 'gurk' or something like that. 'I have a bad case of gurk,' he complains—"

With a shout of laughter Henry threw the entertaining publication aside, made a great leap around the table, and hugged his wife to him.

"Oh, Gussie, you do make my life such a joy! This *gurk*—I may just have to try it . . . you little temptress—"

"Well, it will have to wait," Gussie pronounced calmly. "I see Matthew coming through the gate."

"Foiled again!" Henry, sock-footed, went to meet his friend.

Matthew laid aside his hat and took the chair proffered by his host. Gussie, impatient for any news concerning his letter to Hannah, studied the dark eyes and splendid profile for some indication of the progress of his long-distance suit. The once-wild boy and arrogant young man had mellowed, with the passing of years and the shaping of circumstances, into a thoughtful, restrained man who was, in spite of his doubts, a man to be prized.

Would Gussie entrust the happiness of her friend to any less than the best? Never!

Matthew was pointing out to Henry the features that made his tethered horse such a prize. The terminology meant nothing to Gussie, and she busied herself in building up the fire in the range, setting the sugar twists into the oven, and arranging the tea plates and teacups from her Imperial Dinner Ware. Agonizing over her dowry purchases, she had been swayed by the warning "The Napoleonic and Trilby fads are dead." The latest fad, it seemed, and by far the handsomest of the many beautiful designs in fine dinnerware, was "The Imperial" from England. Its beautiful design was in olive green, heavily traced with gold, and was guaranteed to please the most fastidious.

Probably not the most fastidious, still Gussie was proud of her 100-piece dinner set, although sadly—and in consideration of the costs involved and the long distance they must be shipped—she had resigned herself to foregoing the 124- or even the 112-piece set, with their additional pieces (could one, she wondered, really *exist* without a *slop bowl?*).

Now, setting out what she needed with which to serve her company, Gussie opened the plush-lined case containing the set of fine silver-plated ware that had been Hannah's wedding gift. Lifting out the teaspoons and sugar shell, she wondered uneasily if she had ever mentioned to Matthew Hunter that the set, with its fancily engraved "C," had come from a fashionable emporium by the name of Vaughn—the same Vaughn to whom he was writing, all ignorant of her status and wealth, for the purpose of asking her to forsake it all and take up a life in the backwoods. What if he put two and two together . . .

Gussie felt a small rush of panic. Turning quickly, she burst into the men's talk with the question, "Matthew—have you heard from Hannah?"

Into the silence that pervaded the room, Matthew turned his face toward Gussie.

"She's agreed to come."

And a smile lit the scarred face.

13

DIGBY SET THE BRIMMING, FROTHY PAIL OF MILK on the table. Dovie waddled—purely and simply waddled—over with the strainer. Above the apron stretching over her middle, Dovie's eyes were alight with life and with love.

Seeing both, Digby counted himself a blessed man and said gently, "I'll strain it, Dovie," and held the clean cloth securely around one side of the pail, hefted it, and poured the morning's milk into the separator's shining steel bowl.

In many such ways Digby saved his little, pregnant wife from overextending herself. So full of bounce and the joy of life, Dovie had miraculously, it seemed to her husband, with resolution put behind her the so recent grief over the loss of two babies and looked with expectation toward the happy delivery of the new arrival.

That it cost her a great deal to do so, Digby knew. And knowing how much having a baby meant to her and how desperately she felt that time was running out, Digby, who would have been happy with Dovie alone for the rest of his days, battled for peace in his own worried heart.

Digby handed the empty pail to Dovie, who took it to a pan of sudsy water and began washing it.

"Butter-making time?" Digby asked, noting the churn that Dovie had pulled from the corner of the kitchen to the side of the table. "I suppose you want me to take it to Meridian with me tomorrow."

"I want to keep on top of things," Dovie explained. "And there's quite a supply—if you'll get it up for me." Dovie referred, of course, to the well-cooled can of previously separated cream awaiting the moment of churning.

"Lovie," Digby began, speaking the word that always melted her heart from the first moment he, a middle-aged widower, had spoken it to her love-starved heart, "I don't think you should do the churning. If we had one of those other types—the cylinder, perhaps, or the barrel—but this dash is very vigorous work. I wish you'd wait until this evening, love, and I'll do it. Or your sisters—will they be coming over today?"

"No, I was thinking of going over there, Digby."

Digby looked alarmed. "But you've been staying pretty close to home."

"Where would I be in better hands, if anything happened, than with my sisters? Anna is the district's midwife—and doctor . . ."

And Dovie picked up Digby's rough hand and cradled it and the scar from the terrible wound that had, after all, been the thing that had brought to fulfillment the love between them.

"You might not be here today if it weren't for Anna." Dovie shuddered to think of it and of the unfolding life for herself that she might have missed if Digby, *dear* Digby, had not submitted to the ministrations of the Snodgrass "girls."

"True enough," Digby said, taking a moment—and then more than a moment—to wrap the precious little form to himself, lay his chin on her head, and know she was listening with little sighs and cries of pleasure, as always, to the beating of his heart. That it beat for her and her alone, she knew. And knowing, she thanked God.

"I have to trust you about this decision, Dovie," Digby said eventually. "I would urge caution—"

"Digby!" Dovie said, laughing up at him. "I'm a farm girl—remember? And tough as they come."

Digby, savoring her softness, could have argued. Instead, he laughed with her, loosed her, and said, "When do you want me to have the buggy up for you?"

Dear Digby! Perfectly capable of harnessing and hitching, having done it for all of the 20 years she and her family had homesteaded in the bush country after leaving their beloved England, she relished Digby's protection and care. Oh, that her twin, Dulcie, might know the same! But Dulcie strongly resisted her sister's matchmaking efforts, still scandalized with Dovie's boldness in the wooing of Digby Ivey.

"But it was all for Anna!" Dovie had often protested when faced with her twin's incredulous exclamations.

"But Anna wasn't interested, was she? And Digby was, wasn't he?"

"And so would Morton Dunn be, if you'd let me—"

"Stop it, Dovie!" And Dulcie, once again, would put her hands over her ears, stamp her little feet, and declare she was perfectly happy and content to remain as she was and to spend her days with Anna, and now Shaver, Digby's son.

"And besides," she reminded her sister, "soon we'll have the baby to keep us busy."

The baby. Yes, the baby. Dovie marveled at how life had changed for her: a loving husband and now—a dream, never dared to be considered for 40 years—a family of her own. Yes, life would be richer for all of them with the baby.

When Crispin the Courser (Shaver had been caught up in medieval history and knights and jousts when the colt was born) was at the door, Digby gallantly heaved and helped, and Dovie and her numerous packages were hoisted onto what seemed to be a very slender step and into a tipping buggy.

"Are you sure—"

"Positive. I'm fine, Digby!"

"I'll be stringing wire—"

"I know where you'll be. Now don't worry, Digby. I feel fine; in fact, I feel—I feel *extra* good today."

Dovie drove sedately out of the yard. The beauty of the morning spoke peace to her soul. Surrounded by such beauty and filled with such peace, it was only natural a prayer would well out of her heart: *"Suffer the little children to come unto me. . . ."*

Not more than a mile down the road, Dovie came to the Runyon brothers' farm, still called that although Willie Tucker had married Hubert and Harry's grandniece and now lived with her and her son, Simon, in one of the lookalike houses that had been built by the brothers in earlier, much earlier, days.

Not having seen Hubert and Harry for some time, and confident it would be some time before another opportunity presented itself, on a whim Dovie turned Crispin and the buggy toward the houses.

Like a flower in her own garden, Sarah rose from her knees at the approach of the rig and met Dovie in the yard.

"How nice to see you, Dovie! My goodness—I didn't expect you'd still be around!"

"Any time, Sarah! Any time now! In fact," she said, reaching a grateful hand for Sarah's and extending a foot that she couldn't see in a search for the iron step, "I feel *extra* good today."

"Oh, oh! You know what that means, don't you?"

Huffing and puffing, Dovie finally stood on solid ground. "No, what?" she asked, alarmed.

"Nothing bad," Sarah soothed. "It's just that mothers-to-be get this surge of energy right before the birth. I remember," Sarah said as she walked with Dovie toward the brothers' house, "scrubbing the floors and baking up a storm the day Simon was born."

Not having carried her previous two pregnancies to

full term, Dovie considered this good news. "Well, good! I'm ready. Everything is ready. Little number C can come any time."

"Number C?"

"You probably don't know it—but the first baby, a boy, we called Abel. Little Bernard was next," Dovie said softly. "This one," she brightened at the cheering thought, "will be Charles. We didn't plan it that way—it's just worked out like that."

"How convenient! The next one can be D for Digby."

"There won't be another one, Sarah. My age is against me, and Digby—Digby has set his foot down. That's why—that's why," Dovie's brave voice quavered, "this is so important."

"We're all praying, Dovie," Sarah said earnestly.

Opening the door, Sarah called, "Old dears—it's Dovie come to call," and turned back to her gardening.

"Don't get up," Dovie said quickly, while in truth the faint scrabbling of the old men's slipped feet was far from accomplishing that courtesy. They sank back gratefully into their ancient rocking chairs, cushioned for them years ago by Bessie and Virgie, the sisters they had married and with whom they had lived so many happy years in the raw surroundings of the bush.

"Dovie, is it?" queried Harry.

"Pull your specs down off'n your head, Harry, and you won't have to ask such iggorant questions!"

"I put 'em there so's I won't have to look at your wrinkled phiz all the time, Hu." Harry responded mildly, nevertheless full of joy that an occasion had arisen that allowed for some good thrust and parry with his brother. For the brothers, it was one of life's pleasures.

Realizing this, Dovie waited, enjoying the moment, knowing it was one of the reasons she had stopped by.

Taking a chair alongside the heater where the old men reigned summer or winter, with or without a fire, Dovie cleverly prodded along what seemed to be a dying subject.

"You're the youngest, aren't you, Uncle Hubert?"

"Say, that's right! That means that your phiz is worse off than mine, Harry. In fact," Hubert said as he adjusted his own spectacles and peered at Harry, "you look uncommonly like a prune."

While Harry spluttered happily, Hubert turned his inspection on his guest. "And you, Dovie my dear, look uncommonly like a plumped-up plum!"

"Thank you," Dovie said modestly, smoothing her dress over her so-ripe middle and just as happy as Harry.

"When's the happy occasion to be?"

"Any minute now."

Harry and Hubert, both childless, looked alarmed, and Dovie laughed merrily.

Somewhat relieved by the sound, the brothers relaxed. Leaning conspiratorially toward his guest, Harry said in a low tone, "We're livin' for the day you-know-who has a you-know-what." And his rheumy eyes flicked toward the other house and Sarah. Harry's delicacy in the matter of reproduction and childbirth seemed incongruous in the bush. But good Queen Victoria's influence had touched even this remote area, and Dovie appreciated Harry's attempt at circumspection in such an intimate and personal matter.

"You see," he continued, "that will make us great-granduncles."

"Harry, you old nincompoop, you mean grand great-uncles!"

And the two sparrers were off and enjoying the best skirmish they had had in a long time.

Dovie almost hated to interrupt. But time was getting away.

"Uncles—uncles," she said soothingly, "you'll both be grand, and you certainly are great."

Somewhat mollified but not quite sure who had come

out winner, the men subsided. Not being fully resolved, there was the happy probability that the discussion could be picked up again. Like a tidbit saved for a hungry moment, Hubert and Harry stored the pleasant possibility away for a more convenient time.

Looking fondly at the shabby Bibles (Bessie's and Virgie's) lying near at hand, Dovie asked, "Any words of wisdom before I take off, uncles?"

Hubert and Harry, for years too busy (and "iggorant") for spiritual things, had left that part of life to their wives. Now the flame burned in them, and burning, warmed the hearts of all who came by. And come by they did; it seemed miraculous, they often said, marveling how God did send people to them—for encouragement, for prayer, and yes, for counsel. Behind their scanty hair worked shrewd brains, and inside their caving chests, caring hearts.

"You show her, Harry," Hubert suggested and couldn't resist adding, "After all, you finally got your specs in position."

Ignoring his brother's sly jab, Harry's old fingers fumbled among the well-marked pages of his Bible.

"Listen to this, Dovie: 'Weeping may endure for a night, but joy cometh in the morning.'" The familiar verse, new to the old men, rang with fresh meaning to their "congregation" as they expounded the Word.

"Now Hu and me—we've done our share of weepin'."

"We seen us a lot of nights."

"Dark and long nights, Dovie. You can't live to our age and not know what the psalmist is talkin' about."

Or my age, Dovie thought.

"But keep your eyes on the mornin'! We'll see Bessie and Virgie—in the mornin'!"

And I'll see Mama and Papa, Dovie thought, *and little A and B!* And her heart leaped at the truth, already known but filled now with a God-given sense of reality.

After prayer, Dovie took her departure; her eyes, and Hubert's and Harry's, were wet with tears and alight with the hope that was indeed "an anchor of the soul, both sure and steadfast."

Driving down the road, how could Dovie know the desperation with which she would cling to that anchor? Or to the strong consideration that sustains those who flee "for refuge to lay hold upon the hope" set before them?

14

WITH THE MORNING SUN A BENEDICTION, SHIN-
ing through the church windows and touching the
heads of the worshipers, Hannah sang, bowed, prayed,
and read on cue. But listen? Her mind, if not her heart, was
a thousand miles away.

Sadly unable to differentiate between human love and
divine, she sang "O Love That Wilt Not Let Me Go" as an
unwilling (even unknowing) skeptic. For never had she
fully rested her weary soul in that love, never having trusted it; never had she experienced life to be "richer and
fuller" in its "ocean depths," never having known it in its
human form. Such love was beyond her comprehension.

The "Joy" of verse 3 she—mistakenly, of course—
equated with the hollow hope that joy might, after all, find
her, even in the almost unbelievable commitment she was
contemplating—more than contemplating—*committed* to
making. For the letter forever sealing her future lay in the
drawstring bag at her side.

She didn't need to read it again; she knew it by heart.
She could see it—every word, every line, every turn of a
letter, a splatter of the ink where the nib had caught. All,
all, she could clearly see in her mind's eye. The only thing
missing was the face of the writer. The log house she could
visualize, the body of a man bending over a table; she
could almost hear the tick of a clock, the scratching of the

pen, the breathing of the one who wrote. But the face eluded her.

What did it matter? He would have to take her as she was—plain. Something in her shrank from the thought of that first moment when Matthew's eyes would light on her, searching, perhaps, for some trace of beauty, of worthiness, in her bravely lifted face. For that it would be lifted bravely she was determined.

And what would *she* see? Pray God it would not be a backwoods Adonis! Pray God it would not be another such face as her father's—arrogant, self-assured, imperturbable, handsome. With that unfading picture in her mind, could she allow Matthew a chance of being amiable, tolerant, considerate? Even this much—without the joy—would be enough! It was all she could ask for, it was what she passionately prayed for:

> *O Joy that seekest me thro' pain,*
> *I cannot close my heart to Thee.*
> *I trace the rainbow thro' the rain,*
> *And feel the promise is not vain*
> *That morn shall tearless be.*

That God's love and God's joy could be like the congregation sang, apparently experiencing them, she supposed. But man's? Knowing neither, Hannah's throat closed over the words painfully, and the song rang on dull ears.

From across the aisle, Pansy gave Hannah a brilliant smile. Pansy, along with Gussie, had no doubt that happiness and fulfillment lay ahead through the doors of marriage. Pansy would be over later to help Hannah with her packing—not a chore to Pansy, but an exciting preamble to Hannah's exciting future.

Brought back to her present surroundings, Hannah noticed ruefully that Delbert had quickly and satisfactorily replaced her on the flower committee. The arrangement of fresh garden blooms was ample evidence that already life here in Mayfair was proceeding without her. Karl and his son, Peter, had the emporium well in hand; Tilda and Malachi could foresee no problems with Vaughn House's care and upkeep. They might even, Hannah supposed, relish the freedom of having no one to please and the pleasure of enjoying only the company of each other. No, nothing would fall apart here; she fancied everything might even prosper.

Just what the future held, for the store and for the home, Hannah was not clear about in her thinking. That it might all be held in reserve, waiting, watching, for the failure of her new undertaking (function, occupation, transaction, profession—what could she call it?) was a thought that, lurking in obscurity, dare not totally reveal itself.

And if she felt a pang of guilt about her decision to say nothing to Matthew about her money and her possessions, that, too, was hastily buried away.

Shaking hands with Delbert at the door of the church after the service, he held her hand longer than was necessary and, looking down into her face with a hint of uncertainty, wished her well.

"Are you quite sure—" Delbert kept his voice low—as if, Hannah thought, those in line didn't know very well that it had been expected that the minister would make her his wife; and as if now all of them didn't know she was soon leaving town—and to be married! Well-wishers waited with outstretched hands and assurances of prayers and requests for correspondence.

"Quite sure, Delbert."

"I understand," Delbert said humbly and, congregation or no congregation, drew her into his embrace.

"To think," Hannah thought with some irony, "Delbert's one and only display of affection was reserved for his good-bye!"

"I wish you well, Hannah," Delbert said warmly. "Count on my prayers for your new—ah, undertaking." He, too, didn't quite know what to term Hannah's future.

Pansy rescued her friend from the inundation of

farewells and congratulations and questions and, arm in arm, they made their way to the Roop home for a final Sunday dinner together. Buell, bringing up the rear with the baby in his arms, let the two have the time to themselves.

"Did you ever?" Pansy harumphed. "That Delbert! He doesn't know a good thing when he sees it!"

"Be easy on him, Pansy," Hannah said with a laugh. "I'll not have him blamed for what is as much my fault as his."

"He's just so heavenly-minded, I suppose," Pansy said thoughtfully, "that he's no earthly good."

"He *is* a good man—a very good man. Come, let's put all that behind us for this last day we have together."

"Maybe we could even thank him," Pansy said tentatively. "His indecision, after all, helped you make up your mind. And I feel sure," Pansy was positive, "this incredible thing you're doing is chock full of possibilities. Think, Hannah, just think—"

And Pansy went into raptures over the romantic aspects of this—undertaking (Pansy didn't know what to call it either).

"Romance, Pansy, is the least part of it," Hannah protested. And while her friend chattered on, Hannah went over in her mind the familiar letter—a far from romantic letter:

Dear Hannah:

Your letter received with its confirmation regarding my proposed offer of marriage. Thank you. I shall spend my life seeing to it that you have no reason to regret your decision. And to doing my best to provide you with the necessities of life and eventually, God willing, some comforts.

That you will be an able helper in all of this is a source of encouragement to me. Together we shall join the brave people of the northwest as they tame this wilderness.

Naturally, I shall be responsible for all costs involved. I have inquired at our station concerning the price of your ticket and that amount is enclosed. Unless detained, please arrive on the 14th of the month. I shall be there to meet you. The wild rose now being in bloom in abundance, I shall put one in my lapel for your identification.

                              Sincerely,
                              Matthew Hunter

"Don't tell me," Pansy pursued her thought, "that it isn't romantic to wear a rose in your lapel!"

"Would you rather he put milkweed in it? For heaven's sake, Pansy!" Unspoken was Hannah's cry, "Don't get me expecting something of the heart in all of this! Don't! Don't!"

"His—Matthew Hunter's—mention of providing some of the comforts, Hannah?" Pansy's tone was amused. "And sending the fare! If he only knew—"

Hannah bit her lip. Her secretiveness—it mustn't backlash and become a threat to her chance for happiness, if not for love. Uneasily she wondered if, after all, she was doing the right thing by keeping her financial picture a secret. But she just had to—there was no option! Rather a single life forever than a—an arrangement that was bought. A pump that had to be primed—no thank you!

As full of possibilities for eventual trouble as it was, it was better to take the chance and say nothing than to reveal her wealth and suspect forever after that it had been much more attractive than she.

"He doesn't know—and he mustn't know," Hannah said aloud now.

"Well, I hope," Pansy said thoughtfully, "he isn't hiding something too."

Hannah, startled, considered the uncomfortable possibility.

❋   ❋   ❋

Matthew turned his horse into the meadow, watched

it kick up its dainty feet and trot, neck arching, toward the others.

Following church he had waited until the crowd thinned to approach Gerald Victor.

"Pastor," he began, "may I have just a word—"

"Certainly, Matthew." Gerald Victor followed his parishioner into a corner of the schoolroom and gave him his full attention.

"I've been writing to a friend of Gussie Chapman—"

"I wondered if you'd share it with me, Matthew," Gerald said with a smile.

"You know—"

"Surely, Matthew, you know the district well enough by now to know it was a distinct possibility. In fact, it's of such interest that I've no doubt it has spread like wildfire."

"Gussie, I suppose."

"Well—Gussie, by means of the Snodgrass sisters, I should suppose. We live a sheltered life here, Matthew . . . and a bachelor of your reputation—" Gerald Victor smiled.

Matthew sighed. "This is one, shall we say, 'conquest' that isn't like all those others. This one will be based on reality."

"Reality, Matthew?"

"This girl—woman, Hannah Vaughn, hasn't seen me—"

"And you haven't seen her," the pastor reminded gently.

"Well, true," Matthew said with some surprise. "I guess I've been thinking of it from my perspective. You've been here long enough to know my, er, reputation, as you so kindly put it."

"You were young, Matthew, full of ginger."

"Yes, and taking everything for granted. I'd like just one relationship—marriage, of course—that's based on honesty, mutual respect, sincerit—"

"Quite a list! I take it, then, you've told her about your accident?"

Matthew's bronzed face turned a dull red. "Well, no. You see, I want to have her reaction in person—not turned down by letter in response to an explanation and a description."

"Is it fair?"

Matthew was silent. "Probably not," he admitted. "But I have to know—will she accept me as I am? I think I'll know—I don't think a woman can hide any feeling of revulsion."

"Revulsion, Matthew? Surely you speak too strongly!"

"Not really," Matthew said stubbornly. "I've seen people's reactions. Girls who found me irresistible," he said as he grinned, but his tone was serious, "were suddenly far less smitten than they had let on. It was a life-changing accident, Pastor!"

"Well, Matthew, you're an adult—and now a praying adult. I'm sure you've made this a matter of serious prayer."

"Of course—almost without ceasing, as the Bible says. If you'll pray with me—and for me—"

"Of course." And pastor and parishioner bowed heads and for a few moments earnestly asked for the Lord's will in the matter.

"You wouldn't have any objection to performing the ceremony, Gerald?"

"If she's as thoughtful and as certain as you seem to be, I'd be happy to."

Now, thinking of the arrangements, Matthew found his heart quickened. Would this Hannah be the quality of person her friend Gussie insisted she was? Had he made a mistake by not forthrightly explaining how his injury had changed his life—not only physically but emotionally and spiritually? And how he had come to see himself—not adequate in himself but much in need of finer traits. The knowledge had sent him to his knees, there to find cleansing and—for all time—acceptance. Even now he thanked

God for it and wouldn't exchange the new life for the old for any price.

And so he had written of surface matters; time enough, when Hannah arrived, to reveal the intimate matters of the heart and mind. *If* she had a heart and a mind to hear; Matthew faced the sobering possibility that this unknown person could be a shallow, frivolous person.

But he was committed. What he had offered he would stand by. Would she?

Time would tell. Matthew turned toward his small house and his lonely meal to glance around at the simple furnishings, many of which he had made, the comfortable dwelling, built by his own hands and to his own design, and found it satisfying.

This—and a marred face and a whole spirit—was what he had to offer.

Would it be enough?

15

"MORNING! TIME TO GET UP!"

When Elsie Crabbe opened the bedroom door on the sleep-drugged children, it was to find Neddy on his pallet and Holly in the double bed.

"Come, children. Breakfast is ready, and I need to get on with my day's work."

So saying, the woman once again pulled the door shut, and her steps could be heard going down the carpetless stairs.

"Oh, say!" she called back, pausing. "Be sure and make up your beds!"

It had been a long time since Holly and Neddy had slept in a "really truly" bedroom. The wagon on the trail had been their sleeping quarters during bad weather, and in good weather they had either pitched a rather raggedy tent or simply slept under the stars. Rose, a true pioneer at heart, had adapted readily and had made it fun for her family.

"It'll be worth it all—you'll see," she often said, "when we get to Wildrose."

And truly the name beckoned. Much more, they decided, than Yorkton or Estevan or even Moosomin. The colorfully named lakes and areas of the north were too distant and too scantily populated to attract them—Lac La Ronge, Cree Lake, Lake Athabasca. Swift Current, Moose

Jaw, Duck Lake, Red Deer Hill—now those were enticing names to Edward and to Neddy, who tended to side with his father.

"But Wildrose is so—so descriptive of both the rawness of the territories, and so—so promising of what life might become for us," Rose had explained, and Holly, tending to side with her mother, agreed.

But she woke this morning to a vista, from the bedroom window, of vastness as far as the eye could see. Grass, grass, and still the grass went on. Mr. Crabbe, already heading into the horizon, seemed a speck for size. In the early morning heat, he and his rig danced in the wavering rays of the sun.

Life on the frontier was harsh, as harsh as the pitiless picture framed in the window of the isolated house. Interrupted only by railway lands, school lands, and in some places Hudson's Bay Company lands, the pattern of the homestead lands dispersed settlers and guaranteed a life of isolation.

In areas where farms were smaller than here on the prairies, neighbors were closer. Though hidden often by the bush, one always knew another human being lived within reasonable distance and could be reached in case of emergency, and fellowship could be maintained in those rare moments of socializing.

Here in particular the winters were to be feared. There would be rest from the effort of making land and harvesting crops, but there would be the endless weeks of cold, the fear of accident, the anxiety over diminishing food supplies. Blizzards raged, with loss of stock and, at times, human life, leaving a family helpless and forsaken in the teeth of the blinding storm.

All this Holly understood, some of it instinctively, and her gaze lifted northward—but encountered only haze and heat.

"What'll I wear, Sissy?" Neddy was asking, and Holly

turned from her survey of their surroundings to search out some clean clothes for her brother and herself.

"Are you coming?" came a sharp call from the foot of the stairs.

Holding Neddy by the hand, Holly descended the steep, narrow stairs, passed through the front room, and entered the kitchen. Here, as in all kitchens, the range reigned, queen (and slave) of all. This one, as most, was obviously its owner's pride and joy: it was black where it should be black and shiny where it should be shiny, without rust or corrosion or splashes of food. On one of its six lids a pot simmered.

"Oatmeal—," Neddy muttered resignedly.

Holly tugged warningly at his hand.

"Hoity-toity, is it?" Elsie Crabbe said, giving the child a pained glance. "Nothing so fine as that, I'm afraid. Looking around that camp of yours, I wonder that you had anything so expensive as oatmeal. No, young Edward, it's boiled wheat. But never mind—" She passed a conciliatory hand through Neddy's red-gold curls. "We'll do better for supper. That is, if Syl comes home with prairie chickens."

"Where has Mr. Crabbe gone?" Holly asked politely, sitting down at the oilcloth-covered table.

"To the herd. You wouldn't know, I'm sure, but cattle ranching is becoming big business. Have you heard of Sir John Lister-Kaye? No? He started it, I suppose, when he purchased all those acres, 100,000 of them, distributed mostly along the Canadian Pacific railway west of Moose Jaw."

Elsie expertly plopped several generous spoonfuls of the boiled wheat into the two bowls on the table.

"This was for the purpose of raising pigs and sheep and cattle and horses." Elsie pushed the milk toward Holly and began adding brown sugar to Neddy's wheat.

"Actually, Mr. Hoity-toity got his comeuppance in '95, and though his operations are continuing, they can't last long."

"How did he get his comeuppance?" Holly asked, interested in the unfortunate Sir John Lister-Kaye.

"Fires, hail, hard winters. Could happen, of course, to any of us."

Elsie Crabbe sighed, and her eyes, shadowed with a never-fading anxiety, lifted to gaze through the screen door toward the sea of grass that surrounded them.

"Now Pascal Bonneau—heard of him? No? He started a ranch with just four horses and four head of cattle. Already he has nearly 400 horses and 400 cattle. I tell Syl that what Pascal Bonneau can do *we* can do."

Elsie's eyes, a hard blue, were turned in almost fanatic determination on the children. Holly, in spite of herself, shrank against the back of her chair. Neddy, however, was spooning the boiled wheat into his mouth and chewing experimentally. And chewing—and chewing.

"Making headway with that wheat?" Elsie asked. "Well, I do have some toast here." And she turned to the warming oven and lifted down a plate of previously toasted, homemade bread, and the children's eyes widened. Cooking over a campfire for a year or so had made bread and other baked goods a treat indeed.

Elsie was opening a jar of wild plum jam. "Wild plums," she said. "These grow in the brakes and low hills way—way over there."

Holly's eyes flew northward, visioning the distant growth and the vivid fruit.

"Takes a whole day to get 'em. You can help this year when it's time to pick them. *If* you're here. And," she added somewhat heavily, "you will be, of course."

When the toast and jam and boiled wheat and glasses of milk had been disposed of, Holly helped Elsie Crabbe do the dishes and put the things away.

"We ought to settle what you'll call Syl and me," the woman said. "I don't suppose you'd want to say Ma and Pa—"

Holly shook her head, her eyes haunted.

Elsie sighed. "Well, most everyone calls older people 'Uncle' and 'Aunt.' How's that suit you?"

"Fine," Holly whispered. "'Aunt Crabbe'—"

"No! No! Not that!" And Elsie's nostrils flared at the unhappy combination. "'Aunt Elsie.' 'Aunt Elsie' and 'Uncle Syl.' All right?"

Holly nodded. Neddy, seeing Holly nod, nodded too.

Elsie was fastening a sunbonnet onto her head and turning down the cuffs of her gingham dress.

"I have to go out into the garden for a while this morning," she said, "and you can help me. Here, child—" and she handed Holly a faded, shapeless sunbonnet. "Hasn't the boy got a cap or something?"

Holly ran to scrabble among their belongings and came back with Neddy's navy blue, broadcloth paddock cap. What memories it conjured up! Holly could clearly remember the small town with its general store and how Neddy's eyes had fixed on the cap so generously embroidered on the front with gold and silver threads. As if it were yesterday, she could hear her mother laughing as she read, "One of the handsomest and swellish caps we have." Eyes brimming in spite of herself, Holly set the cap onto her brother's head and turned blindly toward the door. But not too quickly for the sharp eyes of Elsie Crabbe.

"Come now—what's this! Haven't we had a good breakfast? And aren't we lucky to have a good home provided for us? Let's have no crying, if you please! Aunt Elsie might get the idea you don't like all this—provided for you and with no possible chance of payment!"

"I'm very grateful, I'm sure, Aunt Elsie," Holly managed with the politeness she knew Mama would want. "But you see—my mama bought that cap for Neddy—"

"And a rare extravagance it was. T'would be better, far, if young Edward had a straw hat. With a brim." And Elsie gave the drooping brim of her own headgear a yank that, perhaps best of all, hid her face from the tight-lipped girl. Criticizing her mama was, without a doubt, the gravest infraction anyone could perform. Only an idea that to raise an objection would call forth another "hoity-toity" kept a rebellious outbreak from occurring then and there.

Neddy proved so listless and uninterested in the art of hoeing, and Holly required so much supervision to keep her from uprooting tender, unrecognized shoots along with the weeds, that Elsie, with a sigh, produced a basket and sent them to gather dandelion greens and lamb's-quarter for the supper table. Not a bit certain what lamb's-quarter looked like, let alone tasted like, but well familiar with dandelions, Holly took Neddy by one hand and, clutching the basket with the other, headed north.

Finally, the bottom of the basket covered, their fingers discolored from the oozing dandelion milk, the children sat down. In their nest, the prairie grasses above their heads, they looked at one another.

"Sissy," Neddy whispered, "do we got to stay here?"

It was the question in Holly's mind.

"For now, Neddy," she said, wiping a trickle of sweat from her brother's cheek. "Now, you put your head on my lap and take a nap while I do some thinking."

The sun climbed, the birds muted their songs, the wind sighed through the grasses, the grasshoppers skipped around them while Holly thought—as hard and earnestly as ever in her short life. Alone, parentless, without money, friends, or hope, Holly lifted her dark eyes under the damp mass of dark hair and looked—ever and always—north.

She was brought to her feet, jolting Neddy awake, by a shrill and distant shrieking.

Elsie Crabbe, catching sight of the head and shoulders rising above the grass, bawled a command: "Get over here!"

Tramping through the growth, Holly and Neddy returned to face a red-faced, obviously relieved and very aggravated Elsie.

"Don't ever *do* that again! Don't you know you could get lost out there and never be found again? I declare!"

Leading the expressionless children into the house, Elsie snatched her bonnet off, collapsed into a chair, and breathed deeply. "You've scared me out of my wits! Now take your hats off, wash your hands, and go sit in the other room while I recover. In a few minutes I'll fix a bowl of bread and milk—"

Apparently overcome with the heat, the fear, and the weight of her responsibility, Elsie fanned herself with her sunbonnet. Holly herded Neddy to the washbasin, flushed guiltily when he left a dark stain on the thin towel, and led him into the other room and the couch. There she entertained him with the catalog and their favorite game: "What would you buy if—"

"If I could," Neddy began when the big book fell open to a page featuring travel articles, "I'd buy you this parasol."

"'Pure silk . . . deep flounce and puff . . . pink, blue, or cardinal,'" Holly read. "Good choice, Neddy! I'd like cardinal, if you don't mind! Now what else would you buy if—?"

"This fan!" Neddy said promptly. "You'd be cool then, wouldn't you, Sissy?"

"I certainly would. See, it's made of 'tinted satin, is handsomely decorated, and is the choice of ladies of this and other large cities.'"

"Oh," Neddy said sadly, "we're far from the city, aren't we?"

"Very far, Neddy."

"Well, then I'd buy you this shopping bag, Sissy, and we could make a trip. What city will we go to, Sissy?"

Holly's gaze had left the catalog with its tantalizing choices. Head lifted, eyes drawn as though by a magnet, she stared unseeingly at a blank wall—a wall that faced north. Where else?

Where else indeed?

16

WITH A FLOURISH, DOVIE WHEELED CRISPIN THE Courser through the gate and into the yard.

"Ahoy the house!" she called gaily.

The sound of their sister's voice and the rattle of the rig were enough to draw Dulcie from the house, wiping her hands on her apron, Anna from the icehouse where she had been skimming cream from several pans of milk, and Shaver, Dovie's stepson, on a run from the region of the barn.

All three greeted Dovie cheerily.

"My—you're looking chipper today!"

"What in the world brings you so far from home?"

"Tea's ready, Dovie!"

Three pairs of hands reached to help the rotund mother-to-be from the buggy. Grasping the nearest, Dovie heaved herself forward and stretched her foot once again toward the iron step poised at the end of a projecting iron bar—stretched and missed.

With her considerable weight behind her leaning body and her foot plunging on past the step, Dovie's bulk inevitably followed. As she pitched down, and forward, her fall was checked when she slammed into the buggy wheel.

Horrified cries rent the air. Six hands attempted to extricate Dovie from the pinioning buggy on one side and the wheel on the other.

Startled by the noise and confusion, Crispin jumped, gouging the iron step into Dovie's shin; the shifting of the wheel scraped her bulky body.

"Shaver! Get the horse!"

Finally, pale and shaken, Dovie was extricated from the dangerous position. Shaver, fully as pale and just as shaken, soothed Crispin and led him away to be unhitched.

With trembling hands the sisters led Dovie into the house and to a chair. There her skirt was hoisted, the bruised leg revealed and exclaimed over, and the extent of her injuries considered.

"I think you must lie down, Sister," Anna advised, and Dovie found herself once again in the room she had shared for so many years with her twin. The tumbled dress was removed and a voluminous gown that had belonged to Mama located and donned.

Dovie, always known for her cheerfulness and a dauntless spirit, tried to smile, but it was a pitiful effort. So much depended on this birth!

A cup of tea was brought; even its restorative powers could not quell the fear that permeated the room, though bravely disguised behind soothing hands and ministering deeds.

"It's clear, Sister," Anna finally said gently, "that it would be folly for you to get up. Digby will have to be told that you need to stay here—at least for now."

"I—I think you may be right. Shaver—"

"He'll go. We'll manage our chores between us, and Shaver can send his father on over and do the chores there. I think, Dovie, we better ask Digby to bring some baby things."

Dovie's eyes flew to her sister's face. "I think you're right," she said, and her hand, lying flat on her bulging stomach, moved convulsively.

Anna's eyes narrowed. "Are you in trouble, Dovie?"

"I'm not sure. Right now I may be just shaken up. Tell Shaver to tell Digby—" and Dovie proceeded to make a list of things she might need and where they were located.

"Don't be too concerned about this part of it, Sister," Dulcie said tenderly. "You know Mama never threw away anything. We have plenty of good clean cloths that will do for nappies and all sorts of woolly wrappings. And all of Anna's medications."

When Shaver was mounted and at the door, Anna intercepted him. "Stop at the parsonage," she said quietly, and Shaver, not misunderstanding, grew white of face and took off at a gallop.

Not a mile from the Snodgrass house, Shaver met the familiar buggy of his pastor.

"Brother Victor!" he said, reining in his horse and interrupting the minister's greeting. "Dovie has had an accident. She fell, sort of, when she was getting out of the buggy. I'm going for my dad now. Anna said I should stop and tell you."

"O my Lord!" the pastor breathed, and it was a prayer. "I'll go right over."

Whipping up his horse, Shaver pounded toward the Ivey homestead and his father.

Digby was on his way in from the fence job and broke into a run when he heard the shouts of his son and saw the horse stretched to the maximum. They met in the barnyard.

"Dovie—," gasped a winded Digby.

"She's had a fall, Dad! Anna said I better come for you. And she asked me to get word to Brother Victor."

"O my Lord!" And it was a prayer.

Shaver slid from the winded horse and followed his father into the house. "Dovie listed some things she thought you should bring—just in case."

With his rough hands sorting among the soft and dainty things, items he had watched Dovie make lovingly through three pregnancies, Digby's throat tightened and his vision dimmed.

"Not another sorrow for her!" he cried inwardly and laid the specified articles into a bag.

When Digby was ready, so was his horse and buggy; Shaver had hitched up and had the rig at the door.

"Don't worry about things here, Dad," he said. "I'll take care of everything. You'll have to do it on the Snod-grass place—you or one of the girls. Which cows are you milking now?"

"Just Curly and Roanie—you know as much about the routine here as I do."

"I'll take care of things," Shaver repeated. "And, Dad—let me know if—when—"

With a promise and a warm squeeze to his son's shoulder, Digby jumped into the buggy, gathered up the reins, and whirled out of the yard—lost to his usually appreciative eye the tranquil beauty of the bush's late afternoon; deaf to his ear the glorious birdsong. For once he took no notice of the height of the grain in the field, did not assess the weight of the developing heads of wheat, and did not compare his neighbor's chances with his own.

Having so recently found Dovie, after nearly 20 years of being alone and raising his son by himself, Digby passionately treasured his newfound happiness. And it was all wrapped up in the unique little person of Dovie. That his happiness had brought such pain to Dovie wrenched his heart with guilt. But along with his groan now came the sure realization that, as well as being the cause of Dovie's pain and sorrow, he was also the reason for what she termed bliss. Digby squirmed, thinking about it, both proud and embarrassed to be so satisfactory a husband—and at his age!

Again the tears threatened—tears that had been held in control during two miscarriages in order that he might comfort and console Dovie. Always before, there had been the consolation of "next time." Now, with that past (and it must be so!), Dovie's happiness was everything. *God! Bring her safely—and contentedly—home to me again!*

Dulcie met him at the door. Her face was strained; her voice, when she spoke, just as strained when she answered his hoarse "How is she?"

Nevertheless, she made an attempt to be—what was for Dulcie equally as unique as Dovie—matter of fact: "I think you may calm yourself, Digby. Dovie is in good hands, you know." Her mystifying facial expressions seemed to flash glances toward Anna and heaven.

Handing the bag to his sister-in-law, Digby hurried to the side of his wife.

"Lovie—" His use of her favorite term was almost her undoing.

Dovie's chin quivered. As much as one could, from a prone position, she threw herself into the reaching arms. "*Dear* Digby . . . ," she murmured over and over into his shoulder. "I've been a little frightened. But now that you're here—"

Gaining confidence and peace from the strong arms that rocked her and soothed her, Dovie finally loosed herself, leaned back on the pillow, and said with the beginning of excitement, "I think the baby is going to come, Digby. Don't worry! It isn't really all that early. Babies know when to come—I just jogged this one into remembering."

Misty-eyed again, Digby became aware of his pastor, and friend, at the foot of the bed.

Rising to take the warm hand extended to him and resting in the hope that burned unquenched in Dovie's eyes, Digby found his own breath evened and his own calm restored.

"We've been praying, my friend," Gerald Victor assured. "Now I'll leave you two alone—but I won't be any farther away than the other room. If you want me—"

And Gerald Victor settled himself in a comfortable

rocker, there to read and pray alternately throughout a long night.

In due time Anna, between repeated trips into the bedroom, had supper on the table. The cleanup went more slowly; Dovie's pains had begun in earnest. In due time, Dulcie thumped in from the barn with the milk. In due time—

To the waiting (and listening) twin and pastor, the sounds emanating from the bedroom were telling. Dulcie was so in unity with her twin that she seemed to feel every pain, suffer every agony, and was inclined at times to join the cries and groans of the sufferer. With this birth, as with the others, Dulcie had been ejected, kindly but firmly, from the birth scene. Anna, with Digby's help, could manage the job.

But the suffering was intense. The other babies, born too early, had been undersized. Dovie's girth this time hinted at the reason for this longer, more severe, delivery.

"I do declare, Gerald," Dulcie cried, "I can't go through this much longer! What's taking so long?" And Dulcie would again tiptoe to the door, open it a crack, and return to pace the floor more shaken than ever, her groans and her prayers intermingled.

Once or twice Anna came out to stretch her back, breath deeply, get a drink, check on the fire (Dulcie being undependable), and give a report. Digby, faithful Digby, didn't leave his wife's side.

About midnight Anna thrust her head out to ask, "Dulcie, do you think you can pull yourself together enough to make some tea? A little refreshment would be in order, I think, for us and for Brother Victor."

Dulcie's task didn't take long—the water had been kept at a boil for hours, it seemed. With a rattling tray in her hands, she served her pastor and knocked at the door, handing the cups in for Digby and Anna.

"It's dreadful! Dreadful!" she moaned after her last peek. "That *Eve!*" And Dulcie, with heartfelt condemnation, laid the root of the problem precisely at the feet of its instigator—Eve, to whom the Lord said, "In sorrow thou shalt bring forth children."

After a silence—more frightening to Dulcie than the shrieks and groans, marked only by Anna's words of encouragement and Dovie's gasping breath—the rafters rang with a final, piercing ululation that seemed to have been ripped from the throat of the sufferer.

Dulcie, with her hands over her ears and her eyes shut with the horror of it all, completely missed the faint cry.

Only when all torturous sounds had ceased did she slowly remove her hands and look fearfully toward the door. Gerald Victor laid a hand on her arm, and she jerked her eyes in his direction.

"It's all over, Dulcie."

"Over—?" Dulcie swallowed convulsively.

"It would seem we have a baby—you missed its first cry!"

Now it was Dulcie who cried. Collapsing in a plump little heap on the couch, she let the tears flow, again blind and deaf to all proceedings.

And so it was that she jumped, startled, when Anna spoke: "Here's your nephew, Dulcie."

Reaching arms—arms as starved for baby-flesh as her twin's—Dulcie received the warm bundle that was Charles Ivey.

"Is it supposed to be—blue?" she asked quaveringly.

*　*　*

Reaching home with the dawn, Gerald Victor was met by an anxious Ellie. Word of the impending birth had spread, of course, like wildfire through the community.

"Dovie's fine," he said tiredly.

"But—but Gerald—the baby?"

"It's a boy, Ellie. And unless babies are supposed to be that blue, he's in trouble."

Ellie's eyes filled with tears. "Someday—someday," she said fiercely, "we'll all live near a doctor and a hospital, and these babies—now filling our cemeteries—can be saved!"

"In the meantime, Ellie, we mustn't give up. I tell you frankly," Gerald's face was sober, "I don't know how Dovie can take another loss."

"I know—she's been so fixed on that verse—what is it?"

"'Suffer the little children to come unto me,'" the pastor quoted. "And we know she's interpreting it incorrectly. Oh, Ellie, how can I help her through such a blow—how will her faith recover? She's been so adamant, so unmovable from her conviction that this is a word for her from the Lord."

"If she heard correctly, it *will* come to pass, we know that. If not—"

Ellie's face was as somber as her worried husband's.

17

WITH THE CLICKETY-CLACK OF THE WHEELS counting away the few remaining miles, Hannah dabbed at a definite beading of perspiration on her upper lip and faced the fact: she was nervous.

Although her cool demeanor may have hidden it from others, a feeling close to panic threatened to overcome her. All the years of matter-of-fact, calm-and-collected, in-control managership of the store and its many employees availed nothing in this never-before-experienced situation.

Moreover, her old insecurities rose cruelly to rob her of any sensation of pleasure or anticipation, which, one would think, should be the attitude of a bride-to-be.

Hannah smoothed the skirt of her pearl-gray suit, grateful that she had withstood Pansy's indignant (and honest) reaction that she would reject the current style, so readily available through the store, in favor of sheer simplicity.

But all that rustling taffeta, those miles of braid, that gimp and velvet trim! Never! As usual, Hannah had engaged a seamstress, and her traveling costume (which, she supposed, would also be her wedding dress, for the ceremony was to be performed immediately) had been made to her specifications.

Assembling the "findings" for the project, Hannah had hardly been able to grasp the thought—her wedding dress!

2 yards Selisia waist lining

6 yards cambric skirt lining (cut to 4 at her com-
    mand—no 5-yard sweep for her!)
2 spools buttonhole twist
1 pair dress shields
4 yards velveteen skirt binding
1 spool silk
1 yard wigan
1 dozen dress steels
1 card of hump hooks and eyes

And the wedding dress was only the beginning. In spite of her determination to be sparing, even frugal, the trunks and boxes filled up at an alarming rate: pocketbooks, boleros, waists, collar and cuff sets, drawers, aprons, chemises, shawls (beaver, cashmere, wool), hose (cashmere, lisle, silk, all wool ribbed for winter), vests (Swiss ribbed, Egyptian cotton, silk, wing arm, long sleeved for winter), union suits (the Princess, the Snow White Venus, the Trilby), gloves, wrapper, mittens (for winter). Shoes—hats—nightgowns—The list went on and on. Eventually she had repacked, leaving much of it behind.

"But, Hannah!" Pansy had argued, "These are just everyday items any woman needs!"

"I mustn't seem—ostentatious," Hannah decreed firmly.

"Ostentatious! The things you *are* taking are all plain—"

"Just like me."

"Oh, Hannah—give yourself a chance!"

"He takes me, just plain me, or he takes nothing!"

In spite of it all, Pansy thought secretly and with an inner smile, Hannah's innate sense of good taste came through. Her things might be free of the popular gewgaws and gimcracks, but they were of excellent quality, a feature Hannah never thought to question, having been used to it all her life. And they fit her tall, slim figure perfectly. Yes,

Pansy decided (but forbore to mention aloud), Hannah had a way of looking queenly in spite of her efforts.

Aside from her personal wardrobe there had been numerous household items to consider; most of them would be left behind. A few of the simpler wedding gifts would be taken; Pansy would have been insulted if Hannah had refused to make room for the Fruit and Vegetable Press and Strainer she had selected after agonizing thought, discarding many finer, daintier gifts.

"I hope it's not too—too—," she had said anxiously.

"It's fine," Hannah had assured her. "And I doubt it's anything Matthew already has."

"It's especially good for mashing potatoes," Pansy pointed out. "Potatoes forced through the strainer are *lump free*."

Hannah obliging worked the handle experimentally and packed the lovingly selected and given gift with something between a laugh and a sob.

All these last-minute details crowded Hannah's mind now. Actually, it had been a relief to say her good-byes—at church, the emporium, along the street, and to Malachi, Tilda, Pansy, and the babies.

"If you need to write," she told Karl, "address me at Gussie's for now." The same advice went to Malachi and Tilda. Pansy would write—and often!—directly to her. "But be careful what you write!" Hannah warned, and Pansy's face had darkened. Pansy was not at all sure marriage should start with secrets. But she fully understood Hannah's determination to be taken "at *face* value."

"No pun intended," Hannah had quipped, serious at heart. "This is one time when my face is truly my fortune—or my pauperism," she added more grimly, in an aside.

But Pansy heard. "Oh, Hannah," she grieved, "you are so much more than your face—as we all are. I wish, just once, you could see yourself through my eyes."

But Pansy's eyes were loving eyes, hence to be questioned. Hannah's father's eyes, uninfluenced by any such emotion, had proclaimed his daughter "plain" and "ordinary."

"One good thing about marrying a stranger," Hannah thought now, wryly, dabbing again at the unladylike dampness on her upper lip, "is that when he meets me he won't expect a kiss!"

Which raised other, more worrying, questions. The beading on her upper lip increased.

* * *

At the Meridian station, Matthew Hunter tied his horse and buggy in the shade of a white poplar, glanced at his watch, ran a hand through his springing dark hair, touched his cheek thoughtfully, and turned toward the station.

All was in readiness at home—as ready as soap and water and elbow grease could make it. Realizing it was a simple home, Matthew knew it was still one of comfort, and he was proud of it. One final prayer before leaving it had committed the coming hours and days, weeks, months, and years to the Lord.

There would not be room today, he supposed, for her luggage; it would be safe in the station house until he could return for it with the wagon. This first ride, he determined, would be in style, and he cast a satisfied glance back at the handsome horse and spanking rig.

Thankfully there had been a rain in the night; the roads were free of dust and the bush was at its early-summer best. Any right-minded person would recognize its beauty! Yes, he had a few good things in his favor. And again he touched, lightly and thoughtfully, his cheek and the wound that had catapulted him into such an unusual situation. Pray God Gussie hadn't deceived him! That Hannah might be (was!) deceived was an uneasy thought. But it was a necessary part of his plan!

Taking a snowy handkerchief from his pocket, Matthew wiped a beading of perspiration from his upper lip.

When the huffing, puffing monster pulled to a screeching halt, Matthew nonchalantly tipped his derby to the back of his head, slipped his thumbs into his vest pockets, and walked to the area where, he supposed, a passenger would disembark.

Stepping down at the opposite end of the carriage, Hannah's eyes flew along the platform. Without a doubt the one male in a suit, obviously watching for a passenger, was Matthew Hunter. And yes—the promised wild rose was in his lapel. Head tipped back, suit neat, posture casual, Matthew was the picture of masculine appeal, and Hannah's heart sank. She didn't know what she had expected—but certainly not this well set-up, clean-cut, vigorous personification of manhood.

What had possessed such a man to *advertise*—write for a wife! Briefly, honestly, she supposed it might be for some of the same reasons she—an intelligent, capable, *moneyed* person—would resort to the same means.

Walking with purposeful steps toward the man so intent on the wrong area, Hannah's dismay increased as Matthew's features came more clearly in focus: high, noble forehead; ruddy, tanned complexion; straight, dark eyebrows under a falling lock of hair; a strong nose—

Hearing the approaching footsteps, Matthew turned, from profile to full face—a strong nose and—a terrible scar.

As long as life remained and he drew breath, Matthew Hunter would bless Hannah for her manner upon coming face-to-face with him for the first time. For it was undoubtedly she; no one else had left the train who could possibly be considered a woman of marriageable age.

With his back to the sun, he was seen chiefly in outline. It was an advantage; it would be a moment before she saw him clearly. A moment in which *she* was starkly, clearly observable. In that moment Matthew saw a slim, graceful figure, gowned in a manner that suited her admirably, her head up, her step sure.

When Hannah stopped in front of him, for a brief minute they looked quietly, honestly, directly into each other's face. Matthew saw dark, fringing lashes around blue-gray eyes, a mobile, sensitive mouth, a small square jaw, and a creamy pallor that, at the moment, was touched with a faint underlying tinge of color—the hint of possible misgivings.

The firm chin lifted in that close inspection, and the unflinching gaze roved his own face as, he supposed, his was studying hers. Wide, frank, her unaffected eyes studied his hair, his eyes, his lips—his injury.

There, at the ugly, twisted, slashing scar, her gaze rested. His own eyes, just as steady, watched—watched and saw, incredibly, the first sign of animation in that carefully set face. Not dismay, not pity, not revulsion; neither did her gaze drop from the sight of the wound hastily, as so often happened, in an attempt to seem to overlook or avoid the disfiguration.

Hannah's eyes, roaming the length of the scar that crooked from the corner of his eye to the corner of his mouth—not a neat scar but one badly torn—softened. Her carefully maintained facade shattered, and her entire face took on a compassion and sweetness that, to the watching man, told a story in itself.

Then Hannah's hand lifted, and with gentle intimacy she laid the back of it against the bitter mutilation. No mother's touch could have been more tender; no sweetheart's care more wordlessly expressive. Just as wordlessly Matthew took the slim hand in his, held it a moment as they looked long and searchingly into each other's eyes, and then slowly he put the hand to his lips and kissed it.

And so, on meeting, Hannah had her kiss after all.

As long as life remained and she drew breath, Hannah would bless Matthew Hunter for his manner upon coming face-to-face with her for the first time.

18

PERHAPS IT WAS THE HEAT. MORE LIKELY IT WAS the shock of losing first his mother and then his father. Neddy, usually so rosy-cheeked and chubby, drooped alarmingly.

"It's this blessed heat!" Elsie Crabbe said at first. But when a cloudy spell didn't seem to make any difference to the boy's lackadaisical manner, she looked into the matter further.

"Perhaps it's worms," Elsie fretted. "Either that or thin blood. He probably just needs a good physicking."

Holly didn't know what that was, but it sounded better than worms. Neddy was sluggishly turning the pages of a book and didn't seemed alarmed by either possibility.

"Holly—climb up on the stool—there, that's it—and get that bottle—no, that sorta shiny one. That's it! Now hand it here."

When Holly had relinquished the bottle into Elsie's reaching hand, she discovered why it was shiny. It was slick with oil.

"Whew!" she breathed and held her hand away from her flaring nostrils.

"Hoity-toity! Haven't you ever smelled cod liver oil before?"

"No! What is it?"

"What is it? My lands, child, but your education is

lacking! It says," and Elsie lifted the bottle into the light of the window and peered at the label, "'This oil is imported from Norway at certain seasons of the year and can therefore be guaranteed fresh and pure—'"

"But how long," Holly asked wisely, "has it been since you bought it?"

"Lands, child! Do you suppose they date these things, with an expiration date or something like that? What an idea!"

"Well, what *is* it?"

"If you'll listen a minute and stop your eternal chatter, I'll tell you. 'It is carefully selected for us,'" she read, "'from the first pressings of the livers of the Norwegian cod—'"

"What's a cod?" Neddy asked, interested at last.

"A fish, of course."

"And they press their livers?" There was incredulity in the small boy's reaction. "I don't think I'd like that, Aunt Elsie. I don't like liver at all!"

"That's why you're puny," Aunt Elsie said triumphantly. Squinting at the bottle, she continued, "'It is an invaluable medicine to those who have weak lungs and are subject to coughs, colds, etc.'"

"I haven't got a cold, and I don't cough."

"I know that, child—I've got ears, after all, and eyes too," Elsie said irritably. "Now let me finish: 'A thin weak person will get stout and strong by continued use, and need never fear of catching cold or having lung trouble, if a little is used faithfully.' Now, little Edward, don't you want to get stout and strong? Like Uncle Syl?"

Neddy, apparently considering the *stout* figure of Uncle Syl, looked doubtful. "I'm just a little boy," he said. "I don't think I want to get stout."

"Mama said—," Holly began.

"Mama, Mama!" Elsie said with a sigh, weary of the refrain, and Holly, looking mutinous, wisely subsided.

"Now, let me see," Elsie said, shaking the bottle,

smelling her own hand and making a face, opening the lid and measuring out a generous draught. "That ought to do it."

She approached Neddy, the spoon extended, as an unbelieving look filled the small, wan face. Neddy cringed from it.

"Sissy—," he cried piteously.

"He's not taking that—that rotten stuff!" Holly exclaimed, pressing Neddy against her thin body.

"Oh, yes, he is, Missy! I guess I know what's best here!"

"It doesn't smell good—it's, it's *rotten!*"

"Just hold his nose, will you? That's what my mother did when I was a girl."

"*You* took it?" Holly's gaze roamed over the slack, gaunt frame with unbelief.

Flushing, Aunt Elsie said sharply, "Never mind that! Just hold his nose!"

But Neddy's nose was pressed into Holly's body, and he rigidly resisted any attempt to turn his head toward the reeking nostrum.

"All right, young man," Elsie said, "you won't get anything to eat until you take your medicine!"

And with a great deal of heavy breathing, she attempted to pour the cod liver oil back into the small neck of the bottle. When done, the bottle was slicker and greasier than ever; it was placed threateningly in the center of the table.

Once again Syl was away for the noon meal. Elsie ate her warmed-over pancakes liberally laced with berry syrup, set a plateful out for Holly, and nothing for the white-faced, big-eyed boy.

Holly sat silently at Neddy's side, and Elsie finally finished off the second plate of food.

Syl, surprised and somewhat perturbed, sat up to the supper table and the rabbit stew, lettuce salad, and biscuits, and listened to an account of the children's defiance.

"Well, listen," he said, "if the boy's undernourished in some way, doing without his food and this good milk won't help."

"It isn't only that, Syl," Elsie said wearily. "It's their stubbornness in doing what I want them to do. How can I be responsible for them if they won't obey me?"

"But is it that important?"

"Just look at him, Syl! The child is sickening before our very eyes! What am I to do?"

Uncle Syl wisely refrained from suggesting that she might take him in her arms. But he did say, "If he's pinin', it's probably for his own ma."

Elsie sighed again. "And I never can be that, can I?"

Uncle Syl sighed too. "Seems," he said, "we've been doin' more sighin' round here than I ever heard before. Beats the prairie wind for aggravation."

"Well, I'm sorry, I must say," Elsie said, aggrieved. "If you remember, I never asked for this job in the first place."

Elsie, bound by her own word and not knowing how to get out of it, watched helplessly as the two children made their way up to bed that night. Unable to escape the remorse, she placed the four remaining biscuits on a plate in the middle of the table, covered them with a cloth against flies, and trusted secretly that they might be gone by morning.

But Holly, relentlessly honest, made no attempt to steal down into the kitchen, though Neddy cried and said his tummy hurt.

Again, in the morning, Elsie broached the subject, at the same time placing a plate of hot buttered toast in plain view.

"Now come on, little Edward," she said, coaxingly and perhaps a little anxiously. "Just take a nip of this medicine, and Aunt Elsie will give you a nice big breakfast."

Neddy shut his lips tightly.

"Too bad," Elsie said, suddenly inspired to use a

trump card. "Yes, sir, it's too bad. Sick little boys can't make trips in the wagon."

"Trips?" It was Holly who responded.

"Uncle Syl is going to the coulee tomorrow—got to have wood. It'll probably be an overnight trip, with camp-fires and all—sleeping under the wagon." Elsie's eyes watched the awakening interest in Holly's eyes. Neddy, the one on whom it all hinged, still looked doubtful.

Elsie dangled the bait a little more. "Bound to be early berries there. A person could play in the water of the little creek—"

"Neddy," Holly said firmly, "take your medicine!"

"But, Sissy!" Neddy felt betrayed.

"Come now—I'll take it first, just to show you it isn't all that bad."

Elsie, astonished at her success, hastily doled out the cod liver oil before either child had a chance to say more. While they were still shuddering, she filled the tumblers with milk and spread jam generously on their toast.

"Now," she said, "it wasn't all that bad, was it? Next time you won't be such a baby about it, will you?"

She wouldn't have counted on it if she had caught a glimpse of the gleam in Holly's eyes.

19

MORNING FOUND DOVIE ASLEEP, HER DAMP HAIR drying in unaccustomed wisps around her face. Digby, curled at her side and still in his clothes, stirred, slipped his arm free, and cautiously rose from the bed. He, too, bore the signs of the night's ravages. His bearded face was weary.

Glancing at his wife's tired face, Digby smiled tenderly. What a little Trojan she was! She should have been the mother of an army; instead, she struggled to obtain one— just one—precious new life.

Having slept for more than two hours, Digby found his thoughts turning anxiously toward the baby. Outside the room silence reigned.

Opening the door quietly, Digby passed into the home's "front" room. Here Dulcie lay curled on the couch, almost as battle-scarred as her twin, but without a baby to show for it. However, any baby of Dovie's, Digby was sure, was a baby of Dulcie's. What a joy this child would be! The entire community would rejoice with them, even as they had suffered with them through two not-so-joyful births.

The word "suffer" brought to mind Dovie's persistent confidence in *her* scripture. In vain had they all, including the pastor, tried to persuade her that she was not indeed "rightly dividing the word of truth."

"Well," Dovie had said, pondering the term, "it may

be that it will be *through* suffering. But God has a baby for me." And she would not be dissuaded.

Remembering the night, Digby thought soberly, "She indeed suffered—poor lass. 'But joy cometh in the morning'!" And Digby tiptoed past the sleeping Dulcie to the attached kitchen.

Opening the door, he was again struck by the silence. But there was activity.

Digby's eyes widened as he took in the perspiring, weary figure of his sister-in-law Anna. So concentrated was she on the task at hand that she failed to hear the approach of Digby.

On the table at Anna's side was a small nursing bottle, with rubber tubing and nipple attached. At her elbow was another bottle; even as Digby watched, Anna tipped it up, poured a portion in her hands, drew aside the swathing blankets on her knee, lifted a small arm, and began massaging it.

Gently, ceaselessly, Anna continued her ministration.

Again and again, as Digby watched, she tipped up the bottle of warm oil, laying aside one small limb and reaching for another, covering them and massaging the child's small chest. Occasionally a faint mewing sound emanated from the folds of the blanket.

Pity for Anna, and a love he hadn't fully known before, welled up in the man's heart as he watched her bent back and realized she had been at this same task ever since the baby had been brought from the bedroom.

Pausing at last to twist and reach toward the open oven of the range and the blanket warming there, Anna caught sight of Digby.

"You might add some wood to the fire," she said into the silence.

Leaning over Anna, looking down at the small body of his son, Digby realized for the first time that something was terribly amiss.

"All is not well, is it?" he asked softly.

He would have sworn that tears filled Anna's eyes. But she answered crisply enough, "He's what we call a 'blue baby,' Digby. His heart can't be functioning properly . . . you can see his color is poor. Of course, he's very tiny. So helpless—"

Digby was right. A tear splashed onto the baby's exposed foot. It was as warm, in its way, as the oil, and Anna methodically incorporated it into the medication and continued her gentle manipulation.

"I'm trying to force the blood to flow," she explained. "I feel," she added in a burst of unexpected helplessness, "so *ignorant!* And so responsible!"

"But you're not, you know," Digby said. "It's only that there is no one—no one at all—who knows better than you what should be done."

"And it isn't enough—it isn't enough. So many times I come away knowing—it isn't enough! Take that injury of Matthew Hunter's—all I could do was draw the jagged lines of that torn flesh together. Every time I look at that crooked seam I blame myself!"

"Anna, Anna! It wasn't a neat cut—his cheek was mangled, remember, by barbed wire. After all!"

Now Anna's tears flowed unchecked. Her anxiety, her night's work, her continual desperate efforts were finally too much. If he could have, Digby would have put his arms around her and let her sob out her frustration and worry. As it was, the baby blocked the way, and he could only pat her shoulder, then smooth her disarranged hair and murmur wordless comfort.

With Anna's tears checked and her task resumed, Digby shook down the grate, poked the coals, and added firewood.

"There's coffee," Anna said, nodding toward the granite pot. "It's old and bitter, but it'll do until Dulcie comes in—"

"Till Dulcie what?" Dulcie appeared, stretching her aching body and yawning. Making for the washstand, she splashed cold water onto her face and washed her hands and straightened her hair before the mirror.

"I need to change," she said. "I'm a mess."

Anna smiled in spite of everything. "You had a hard night, Sister. But you can't go into the bedroom yet—Dovie is asleep. And she needs to sleep—"

"Why—is something wrong?" Dulcie asked sharply, noticing for the first time that Anna was engaged in some sort of work over the baby on her lap, more work than changing a nappie or applying talcum powder.

Leaning over Anna, Dulcie looked at the baby, and her eyes widened. Frightened, she turned her gaze toward Anna.

"Why, Anna!" she faltered. "You're crying—"

Anna, the rock, was crying. It was the most frightening sight of all.

"Digby—," Dulcie cried piteously, as if to say, "Do something!"

"The baby's not doing well, Dulcie," Digby said gently.

"Oh—and I've been asleep!"

"There was nothing you could have done, Dulcie. Now," Anna said with a resumption of her authority, "get some breakfast ready for this new papa. And make some fresh coffee, for goodness' sake!"

It was what Dulcie needed. With a deep breath she plunged into the familiar tasks.

"Should I fix something for Dovie?" she asked, breaking eggs into a bowl.

"Not yet—let her sleep. No need to upset her until we have to. She'll want to have her baby as soon as she wakes up. Perhaps by then," Anna's tone was firm, "he'll be showing better color. Right now I'm going to bundle him up and let him rest for a while. We can take turns later, if need be, doing the massaging."

"You're worn out, Anna! Can't you go to your room

and change—perhaps get a little rest? You can't go all night and all day too!"

"Perhaps later. Right now I need a little coffee. Digby, I should think you can go home if you need to. Shaver will be anxious to know what's happened. Send him on back for his breakfast—and the chores here, if you don't mind. I think I may need Dulcie today."

Anna and Digby had their coffee, their scrambled eggs and toast, while Dulcie kept an anxious eye on the quiet baby. Anna crept away to freshen up, and Dulcie cleaned the kitchen while Digby had a final cup of coffee and kept an eye on his son. So tiny—so frail—so helpless.

"You are loved, little one," Digby said silently, touching the paperlike flesh of the tiny hand. "Get well—for your mother. She needs you so."

The sun was well up when the lamps were blown out and Digby left for home. First, however, he peeked at his wife and breathed a prayer of thanks to find her sleeping peacefully. Dovie—his bouncy Dovie—would bounce back once she had her baby in her arms. Soon they would be home, God willing! But for now they were both in the best care available to them. Giving his thanks to Anna, he told the sisters goodbye and rode for home and the chores waiting there.

Within the hour Dovie called from the bedroom. "Digby! Anna! Dulcie!"

"Go to her, Sister," Anna said, and Dulcie dried her hands and tripped as cheerily as she could to her twin's side.

"The baby, Dulcie?" Half propped up, Dovie's eyes were anxious.

"He's asleep, Sister."

"Bring him to me—and where's Digby?"

"Digby's gone home to do the chores, of course. Life does go on, you know, new mamas or not!"

Knowing her twin as well as she knew herself, Dovie's brows grew together with suspicion.

"I want my baby, Sister."

"Anna and I think you should have your breakfast first, Sister. It's ready, all except scrambling the eggs—"

"The baby, Dulcie!"

Still Dulcie hedged.

"Bring him," Dovie said in a dangerous voice, "or I'll get up and get him."

"Of course, Sister—" And Dulcie escaped to whisper to Anna behind the closed kitchen door: "She wants the baby! She *insists* on having the baby! Oh, Sister—what shall we do?"

"We'll take him to her, of course," Anna said quietly. "Whatever the outcome, we have to depend on Dovie being strong enough to handle it."

Anna lifted small Charles tenderly, wrapped his blankets closely around him, kissed his wrinkled forehead, and walked with calm steps toward the bedroom.

Dovie's arms were out to receive her son.

Anna placed the baby into his mother's arms. Then, stepping to the window, she adjusted the blind, letting in enough sun to create a half-light.

"Higher, Sister, higher. I can't get a good look that way."

"That's enough light for his new little eyes," Anna said practically.

Pulling back the enveloping blanket, Dovie got her first real look at her baby.

"He's so—tiny," she whispered. "Oh, the darling! He looks like Digby, Sister. Don't you think he looks like Digby?"

"A little like Papa, I thought."

"Like Papa! Wouldn't he have been pleased? Do you think, Anna, I should nurse him?" Dovie lifted the fragile hand and inserted her finger into the tiny, clutching fist. "Oh, the darling! Look, Anna—he's hanging on!"

I hope so—oh, I hope so! was Anna's silent cry.

20

WEARY FROM THE TRAIN RIDE, FEELING AWK-
ward about her status as bride-to-be, and quite sure
she looked much less than her poor best, Hannah was
grateful when Matthew bypassed the station and cluster of
curious people and led her toward a buggy and horse.

First, however, he had said with a crooked smile, "You
are Hannah?"

"And you—Matthew?"

"Welcome to Wildrose, Hannah." As he spoke, Matthew Hunter's dark, deep-set eyes were fixed unwavering-
ly upon Hannah's face, as though every subtle expression
was important, as though each shift in thought was to be
analyzed.

Under the gaze Hannah's pearly color—rather than
flushing—paled further. Never had she been so scruti-
nized; never had she felt so exposed. Vulnerable, with
nothing offered but herself, she waited.

Waited and watched. Matthew's expressions, in turn,
were almost absorbed, so sensitively was Hannah tuned to
either his favor or disfavor.

The moment—full of portent for both of them—came
and went. Each in that moment had seen the other as open,
as candid, as artless and free of defenses as they ever
would again in all their lives.

Turning then, with only a deep-drawn breath to mark

its passing, they left the meeting and the moment and started their life together.

Matthew handed Hannah up into the buggy. "I'll get your things," he said, "or whatever you may need for—for the night. If there's more, I'll come for it with the wagon— or someone will. It's the code of the backwoods." He smiled.

"It's a good one," Hannah responded warmly, "and I look forward to learning it and being a part of it."

And again Matthew Hunter's eyes were keen on her face, and his ears, it almost seemed, listened for some deeper message.

With a sudden thought to her secretiveness about her position and wealth, Hannah fought down a small feeling of panic, as if under that listening and watching Matthew Hunter was seeking out the real, the hidden, person she was.

"Yes, there's more," Hannah answered now, "quite a bit of it, I'm afraid. If this is to be a permanent move for me—"

"It is, of course," Matthew said steadily.

"Then it meant bringing everything [everything?] from one life to another." No sooner had she said it than Hannah felt the first pang of misery that she must be so deceptive to this man who seemed to look at her so straightforwardly and honestly. Someday—someday, pray God— she could unburden herself and make a full confession and be understood.

When Matthew had stowed the items Hannah had pointed out to him, he untied the horse, stepped into the buggy with an effortless bound, waved to a few watching people, and turned in the direction of a narrow track. Like a tan ribbon the road threaded the bounty of the bush. The world was sparkling and clean, the fragrance was distinctive and fresh, the birds too numerous to identify.

I feel like Cinderella going to the ball, Hannah thought.

Even Cinderella's coach couldn't have been better drawn than this one.

Aloud she said, "I'm not a great judge of horse flesh, but this one is a beauty!"

Matthew seemed pleased. "You've touched on an important part of my work," he said and proceeded to explain how he had built his herd and that it was beginning to pay off, augmenting his income from the farm.

"Now this one," he said, nodding at the horse between the shafts, "like some of them, was in bad shape when I got her. It's been satisfying to take care of her and see her respond and turn into quite a beauty."

"You're a connoisseur of beauty, Matthew?" The question was out before she knew it.

"I know what I like," Matthew said after a moment in which he was engaged in reining the lively mare to a more sedate pace than she insisted on. "I'm not very often wrong." After another few moments he asked, "And you, Hannah?" still intent on his driving.

"Me?" Hannah was surprised; it wasn't a question she asked herself. "Beauty? I suppose," she admitted. "I think it's important."

Was Matthew's silence filled with meaning? Afraid of it, Hannah added quickly, "My mother always told me 'Beauty is as beauty does.'"

Another thoughtful silence. Did the man always ponder what was said to him? Hannah felt she had gotten herself into deep water—and so quickly!

"Tell me about your mother—your family," Matthew said.

It seemed very strange indeed—here was a man she was about to marry, and he knew nothing—nothing whatsoever, about her.

But then—now Hannah grew thoughtful—she knew nothing about *him*. Or rather, she knew very little, mostly that he loved horses and appreciated beauty.

And he saw it every day when he looked into the mirror. Despairingly, Hannah knew that it was so—the scar could not hide the sheer *beauty* of the maleness that was Matthew Hunter.

From a discussion about their ancestors and their childhoods, their conversation turned to Wildrose—its history, its inhabitants, its hopes. This led most naturally to Hannah's inquiry concerning Gussie and Henry and their setup. Matthew pointed out the homesteads of friends and acquaintances as they went.

Finally, at a spot where the bush had been trimmed back, Matthew pulled the rig aside and stopped.

"Hannah," he said, turning and looking directly at her, "now that you've—you've seen me, and we've had a little time to talk, tell me—"

"Yes, Matthew. I'm quite willing to go through with it," Hannah said, color high at last. "It's what I came for; my decision was made before I left Mayfair."

"All right, then." Matthew pulled the horse back onto the road.

The commitment of each had been made before this hour. All that remained were the legalities.

✱ ✱ ✱

After the excitement of greeting Gussie and Henry, of kissing "Hanky," and being introduced to the minister, Hannah found herself standing on a rag rug in Gussie's small log house, a strange man at her side, repeating the phrases that would link her life to his forever.

"To love and to cherish . . ."

How easy it was, after all, to promise! What woman in her right mind would find it impossible to love a man like Matthew Hunter? But Matthew? Was he able to vow as readily? Glancing up momentarily, Hannah met his eyes; again—that piercing, keen look. Beneath his sun-browned face, however, there was a paleness that belied his rocklike exterior. Whatever his questions, they had been satisfied, Hannah felt instinctively, and knew an instant's surge of something close to relief. It was enough to carry her through the ring given "in token and pledge" of constant faith and to a very real stab of her own guilt through Matthew's ready "With all my earthly goods I thee endow."

In that moment Hannah firmed her decision: no matter the status of Matthew's earthly goods—whether meager or generous—she would be content. Perhaps someday her earthly goods could be disposed of, quietly and secretly, and the proceeds could go to an orphanage or some such charity . . .

"'Those whom God hath joined together, let no man put asunder!' Matthew, you may salute your bride."

When Matthew had chastely kissed her cheek and Gussie and Henry had hugged her warmly, nothing would do but that they must all sit down and partake of the refreshments Gussie had lovingly prepared.

"I can't believe you're really here," Gussie marveled over and over again and kept plying Hannah with the many questions she had concerning folks in Mayfair.

"I almost said 'back home,'" Gussie said, laughing. "People here are always talking about 'back home'; the 'old country' is a phrase we hear all the time. But *this* is home now." And Gussie gave Henry a fond smile. "I hope you soon feel that way about the bush too, Hannah. People either love it or hate it, you know. I always say it depends on their personal situation. Me, now—I'm content."

The long ride, the strange setting, the immediate ceremony—all had taken their effect. Hannah felt almost in a daze, and she wasn't sure it was a happy daze. Far too early to tell that. Rather, it was a numbness from things past, an ignorance of things to come. She was relieved when Matthew pulled a watch from his fob pocket and pronounced, "Chore time."

Of course. She was a farmer's wife now. That chores

should take precedence over everything—even the natural observances of a once-in-a-lifetime experience such as one's wedding—almost tipped Hannah into hysteria.

"Hannah—you're weary!" Gussie remarked. "Of course, it's been a long day. We'll have lots of time to catch up on all we've missed these last years. Oh—I'm so *glad* you're here!"

Gerald Victor was shaking hands with Matthew again and saying to Hannah, "I look forward to getting to know you better and to having you meet my wife. We're rather like one big family here in Wildrose and throughout the bush—wherever people have left everything and everyone behind and stepped out with raw grit and determination to make a new life for themselves. Matthew, now, has made a good start."

"Thank you, Rev. Victor—"

"'Gerald,' please. I hope we're going to be friends. And now, if you'll excuse me—" Gerald turned to Gussie and Henry and explained, "I need to stop by and see Dovie."

"Has she gone home yet, Gerry, or is she still with her sisters?" Gussie was concerned about her neighbor and friend.

"She's still with them. The baby—the baby can't be moved."

Gussie sighed. "So there's no improvement. Do you think I might be able to see Dovie?"

"I think you'd be a great encouragement to her."

Once again it was up into the buggy for Hannah, this time with a thin gold band on her left hand—Matthew's mother's wedding ring.

"This Dovie—," Hannah asked as she and Matthew whirled out of the gate and down the road. "Gussie has written a little—"

"Gussie's neighbor. Dovie and Digby married a couple of years ago—Dovie is over 40, and her greatest desire is to have a family. She's lost two babies, and this third one is not doing well."

"How sad—especially at her age!"

"Right. Digby says it's the last try. He's terribly worried about Dovie. But," Matthew said thoughtfully, "Dovie seems to have come up with some remote scripture—says it's a word from God. We all pray it is."

The beautiful horse, no more sedate than when the trip began, turned of its own accord into a side lane. As they burst from the leafy track into a clearing, Hannah's new home opened before her.

Of log, of course, but not a cabin. Hannah was glad that Matthew had left the wood in its natural state, not whitewashed as many were. It was low, with wide eaves, and spoke of homeyness. Around it were several outbuildings—a henhouse, some sheds, and, at a distance, a log barn. Beyond it the clearing opened to a meadow, then more bush. Fields were apparently hidden by surrounding growth.

"Welcome home, Hannah," Matthew said with warmth and satisfaction and helped Hannah out of the buggy.

From the porch an old dog rose lazily, wagged its tail to add its welcome, and lay back down.

"'Beggar,'" Matthew said by means of introduction, "and a real old-timer. There are several cats around somewhere, all nameless—but needed. We have hordes of mice—hope you're not afraid of mice."

All the while Matthew had been shepherding Hannah across the porch, to the door, and over the threshold.

"Make yourself at home," he said and crossed the room to a door, entered, and set down the bag he was carrying.

Slowly pulling off her gloves, Hannah looked around. The inside was as homey as her first glimpse had promised. Would love blossom here? The warmth and comfort invited it; the silence seemed to wait for it.

The house had been divided in half. The half in which Hannah stood was the kitchen and the living quarters. Thankfully, it was roomy, with its round oak table and matching chairs standing on a colorful rug, a sofa along one wall with bookcases bursting with reading material for long winter evenings, a couple of lamps, one of beauty with its brass base, its shade and illuminator taking the place of the usual chimney and gracefully decorated with a design of flowers, and the second the usual utility lamp.

There were simple curtains at the windows. Two rocking chairs were comfortably cushioned. The walls had been planed until they were comparatively free of irregularities and had been freshly whitewashed. The huge range dominated one corner, and it was surrounded by well-stocked shelves, a dresser, and a kitchen cabinet. There was a lovely buffet along another wall . . . a washstand near the door . . .

The other half of the house had been divided again into two rooms—bedrooms. Each held a bed—one brass, one iron, sturdy chiffoniers, and in one room a battered desk, a desk stuffed with papers, obviously Matthew's work area.

The second bedroom with its pristine coverlet was where Matthew had set her bag. Thoughtfully Hannah removed her hat, laid it on the chiffonier top, placed her gloves beside it, and returned to the other room, where Matthew had stood all the time, watching her silently.

"It's—it's very nice," Hannah said.

"Hannah—" Matthew crossed the floor, stopped before Hannah, took her hands in his, and looked down into her lifted face.

Long and seriously he looked. "I want to say the right thing—do the right thing," he said in a low voice. "This marriage—it's forever. We have all the time in the world ahead of us. I want—," he hesitated, "I want things to be right—for you as well as for me.

"I guess what I'm saying—is that I owe it to you to let

you get to know me. I'd like to think," something—some wound, perhaps, shadowed his eyes, "you could learn to love me. And love, I think, needs time. I've put your things in the second bedroom, Hannah. When you come to me— it will be your choice."

So saying, Matthew Hunter turned, walked steadily across the room and, at the door, turned to add with a smile, "And now I'm going to put the horse away."

If Hannah was feeling any dismay, any surprise, any hint of rejection, it was all made right when, with a lilt to his voice, Matthew said, "If you like, *wife*, you may start a fire in the range and make your husband a cup of coffee."

21

THIS IS A PURE MARVEL; IT IS!" EXCLAIMED HOLLY. "Haven't you ever seen a butter worker before?" asked Aunt Elsie.

"No, ma'am. We lived in town in Ontario. Da worked at a mill, and we didn't have any cows. We bought our butter and our milk and our cream. I never worked butter before."

Holly had helped Elsie with the churning, working the dasher up and down with such vigor that Aunt Elsie had cautioned her not to splash. With the soft butter removed and put in place on the butter worker, Holly, biting her lip in her care not to "make a mess," was engaged in working out the buttermilk.

What was a pure marvel to Holly was spurned by Aunt Elsie with a sniff. "This poor thing? I've been asking Syl for one with a lever, but no—it's either we haven't got enough churning to make it worthwhile or we need to put money aside for a hay tedder."

"Well, you do have an awful lot of grass out there." Holly cast a glance out the window toward the surrounding scenery, her attention momentarily diverted from the task at hand.

"Watch it!" Aunt Elsie squeaked. "You're letting the buttermilk drip on the floor!"

Holly adjusted the "poor" frame of the cheap butter

worker over the corner of the table, lining up the hole and drain over the container on the floor beneath it, and resumed the rolling motion that "worked" the butter clean.

"You need to keep your mind on your work, Miss," Aunt Elsie grunted from the bent position she assumed to mop at the few buttermilk splatters. "I declare—I've never seen such a dreamer in all my born days. Seems you spend more time looking over the horizon than any other 10 people! And there's nothing to see—that's for sure."

"Neddy's out there. I need to keep an eye on him, like my mama always told me."

"He's safe enough, for heaven's sake, my girl! He's watching Syl grease the wagon for the trip tomorrow."

"Are you sure you aren't coming with us?" Holly asked cautiously.

"My land, no! It'll be a relief to have a few moments to myself! Anyways, I've made that trip plenty of times—and will have to make it plenty more. That is, unless you'll go in my place." Aunt Elsie brightened, having found one spot of good fortune in the lot that had befallen her.

"Now it's time to wash it," Aunt Elsie said, suiting action to words and pouring a dipperful over the butter. Holly continued working after Elsie had removed the buttermilk container and substituted the slop pail. "Now—we add salt," she said. "Keep on working it, child."

When the job was done, the butter stamped into the mold, and the worker washed in sudsy water, dried, and put away, Aunt Elsie put part of the fresh butter into the butter dish on the table and another portion into a small jar.

"This is to take with you tomorrow," she said and added the jar to other items she had been assembling— bread, bread knife, matches, cheese, plates, flatware, a sealer of her precious venison—whatever came to mind as she and Holly went through their day. "So's you'll be all ready to take off bright and early," she added. "We'll just have to stick in fresh milk. Have you got your things ready?" she asked now.

"I'm working on it," Holly said thoughtfully.

"You'll need one set of clean clothes," Aunt Elsie said, "and don't forget jackets—it may be cold in the evening. I'll lay out blankets—"

"I'm taking our own blankets," Holly said firmly in the tone Aunt Elsie was beginning to recognize. It was Holly's "hoity-toity" tone.

And in spite of what the woman said, Holly insisted on their own bedding—Mama's quilts and Mama's shawl.

"Shawl? That's too nice to take into the wilderness!"

But Holly's face was mutinous, and Elsie sighed.

"What else have you got in here?" she asked later in the children's room. "Seems an awful lot just for an overnight trip! La, child! Your ma's pendant?"

Elsie picked up the dainty gold wreath of enameled leaves and dangled it by its chain. "And her wedding ring? And what's this? A stick pin!"

Holly quickly took the precious items, and a few others not named as yet, from Elsie's hands, wrapped them back in the scrap of cloth, and thrust them back among her things.

"Well, you're not taking this, for heaven's sake—a Bible?"

"It's my mama's."

"But—to the coulee—to get wood?"

"I—I might read it to Neddy before we go to sleep."

Elsie left the child to her arranging and rearranging, with a shake of the head and another massive sigh.

Searching further, Holly added to her bag her father's knife—its scored ebony handle and wicked six-inch blade safely tucked into its leather sheaf.

All this and more went into the carryall bag she had searched out from the shed where her family's personal effects had been stored. She agonized over the canvas-seated camp stools, the lantern, her father's shaving set, her mother's perfume atomizer, and side combs. Tears sprang into her eyes when she examined a bulge in a pocket of one of her mother's suits and found a small purse and recalled how she had loved to snap its three-ball catch open again and again, counting Mama's coins and listening to the happy jingle of her improvised "toy." Her eyes widened as she automatically snapped the purse open; inside was a handful of coins.

Thrusting them into her pocket, she searched further. Sure enough, in Da's best pants was his pocketbook, with its three small and four regular pockets, its billfold, flap, and strap. Her eager fingers pulled out several bills.

"Oh, Da!" she whispered. "You're still looking out for us!"

Now, relieved that Elsie's prying eyes hadn't seen *all* the items carefully stowed in the canvas carryall, Holly hoisted it, slipped the long straps over her shoulder, and walked across the room and back. Her small frame dragged to the side—and she hadn't added any food.

Now it was Holly's turn to sigh. Reluctantly she removed numerous items—a small music box (she kissed it and laid it tenderly in a drawer with the promise, "I'll send for you!"), a harmonica, Mama's egg darner and waving iron and fancy silk gloves. Left in were camphor cold cream, "a salve of remarkable healing properties," and a bar of soap. A towel! They mustn't disgrace Mama when they arrived at—

Once again Holly turned in her mother's Bible to the scrap of paper she had located earlier: Rev. Gerald Victor, Wildrose, Meridian, Saskatchewan Territory.

One additional thing—a pencil and piece of paper. Checking the hallway to see that Elsie was not near, Holly carefully licked the pencil's lead and wrote:

Dear Aunt Elsie:

Neddy and I are going to find my mother's relative. We will be quite safe and happy there, I'm sure.

I didn't take anything of yors excep some food. Someday I'll pay you back. Someday I'll rite and tell you where we are and ask you to send my da's and mama's things to me. So please keep them safe.

Neddy and I thank you for all you did for us. I'm sorry we were such a great trile to you.

Holly Carroll

P.S. In appriashun I am leaving this new box of carbo wafers, which are a true specific for sour stomach (it says on the box).

WITH THE BUSH BURGEONING SO EXTRAVAGANT-
ly, the gardens flourishing, the grain greening across
thousands of acres and promising its abundant crop, it was
hard to think one small life faded day by day.

Baby birds cheeped from a million nests—in eaves,
grasses, bush, trees, meadow, and slough edge—and rivaled
in volume the faint sound of Dovie's baby. Baby kittens
opened blind eyes, baby chicks fluffed out with new feathers,
colts and calves frisked with strengthening legs, and Dovie's
babe mewed pitifully, paled obviously, and moved feebly.

But no mother hen, tucking her brood under her
wings, no mother cat bird driving away a scavenging crow,
no mother cat cleaning her baby's milky face exceeded for
loving care the ministrations of Dovie to her child.

All around the small Snodgrass home, life went on; inside, time stood still. Visitors came, prayers ascended, tears
flowed, advice was abundant and diverse.

"I tried goat's milk with mine," Dolly Trimble offered,
adding doubtfully, "I don't know anyone in the district
who has goats, though."

"At least a little sugar water . . . ," Grandma Dunphy
encouraged. "The poor, wee babe has to get *some* nourish-
ment." She reported at home, with a cluck, "The child's no
bigger than a bird!"

When Anna's best efforts seemed to no avail, Marta

Szarvas was called in. The mother of 10 sturdy children, the Hungarian immigrant knew by practical experience more about taking care of babies than did many a country doctor. Even Marta's square face grew sober, and she said in her broken way, "Keep his nose passages clear and give him lots of air—he seems to be breathing very shallowly."

"A little, very little, laudanum, do you think?" Maggie Edwards whispered to Anna, and it may have been the best advice of all. It seemed to ease the child's struggle for life itself.

Shaver had been sent posthaste for the doctor, only to come back bleary-eyed, sagging in the saddle, and near tears: "No one knows exactly where he is—out in the bush somewhere. I left word with his wife to send him on."

It was all too little; it was all too late. The little life, so dearly wanted, so dearly paid for, so dearly cared for, weakened almost hourly.

The birth, long and hard, had taken Dovie herself to the brink of the grave; Anna knew this, if Dovie did not. Her physical recovery was slow; it was almost brought to a standstill by the emotional strain, as if, by her very will, Dovie could breath life and health into her baby.

Ignoring all the pressing needs of his farm, Digby stayed with his wife, and Shaver did double duty. But when Shaver reported that a mare was in serious trouble and Digby's expertise was needed to bring her foal to birth, he reluctantly left for a few hours.

"Be a good girl," he cautioned Dovie, kissing her lovingly, "and try and stay down for a while. You can't nurse like you must if your own health doesn't improve."

Dovie, knowing he spoke the truth, and weary beyond all endurance with the birth, the sick-watch, and her breaking heart, agreed.

"Bring him to me," she asked Anna, "and we'll take a nap together."

Anna laid the tiny scrap—so precious to them all—in

his mother's arms and on her bosom and slipped away for some much-needed rest herself.

A blue-bottle droned on the window, a crow called stridently from a nearby tree, the wild roses spread their fragrance from every corner of the bush, and Dovie slept.

Dovie slept, and the babe—slowly, surely, inevitably, peacefully—left its earthly mother's arms for its Heavenly Father's.

It was Dovie's anguished cry, echoing through the quiet house with its terror and grief, that alerted the household.

Anna, hair askew and eyes sunken from her days of unrelenting nurse care, was the first at the bedside. Pulling back the blanket, her tears fell on the tiny, waxen face.

Dovie's sobs grew less hysterical when she saw the grief on the face of her sister, and she tried to comfort Anna.

Dulcie, whose heart beat in tune with her twin's, laid her graying head on her sister's breast and wept. Dovie, the bereaved mother, stroked the dear face and whispered, "Don't cry, Sister. Don't cry."

Then, with unbelievable peace, Dovie laid her baby in Anna's trembling arms and said, "The Lord giveth, and the Lord taketh away; blessed be the name of the Lord."

At this, Dulcie's sobs broke into outright cries. Dovie held the heaving shoulders in a tight grip, laid her cheek on the wet face, and mingled her tears with those of her twin.

And so Digby found them, and his head replaced Dulcie's on Dovie's bosom and in her arms. Reaching his own arms to her, he found, instead, his comfort in hers.

"I don't understand this," he said later to the sisters. "This—this calm—this acceptance—it's unnatural. I'm afraid for her!"

And they watched with fear and trembling for signs of the break they felt must come.

Dovie's pastor came, and he, too, knelt by her bed, taking her hands in his.

"Dovie," he said helplessly, "we can't understand the ways of the Lord—"

"That's true," Dovie agreed, eyes tearing.

"I want so much to help," her pastor continued. "But, Dovie, you know all the promises—God's comfort, His goodness, His love—"

"But, Gerald," Dovie said, breaking in, and there was astonishment in her tone, "aren't you forgetting my promise?"

"Your promise, Dovie?" Gerald Victor was taken aback.

"Surely you remember—'suffer the little children to come unto me—'"

"No, I haven't forgotten. I see its fulfillment, Dovie, don't you?"

"Not yet."

"God took little Charles to himself."

"But that's not what I see in that promise—"

The pastor, plainly troubled and hesitating to ride roughshod over Dovie's recent bereavement, nevertheless felt an urgency about what he saw as her incorrect interpretation of God's Word. Though it might hurt, it would help in the long run, and so he said gently, "Please, Dovie—look at this from the viewpoint of what He has already told us: 'No prophecy of the Scripture is of any private interpretation.'"

Dovie, outmaneuvered by his superior theological knowledge, could only resort to stubbornness. "I know what He told me. And I won't—I *can't*"—Dovie's fervent faith seemed to hold back the despair that threatened to overwhelm her—"give it up!"

The pastor could only bow his head and search for some way to enlighten this misled member of his flock.

"You know, don't you," he said later to Digby and the

sisters, "that she clings to that promise. She believes," and Gerald looked straight at Digby, "that there's a baby in her future."

"I know," Digby groaned. "But, Gerald—there can't be, there simply can't be. Ask Anna—"

Anna nodded. "She can't go through that again. Never! Never!" Anna's voice echoed with the horror of the birth night.

"Well," the pastor said with a sigh, "I can't bring myself to strip her totally of her hope. But, Digby—you're going to have to help her face reality—sooner or later, if she's to have any kind of emotional health."

And Digby tried, with no better success than the pastor.

"Lovie," he said, tenderly stroking her temples and holding her close, "you know you're enough for me. Please let me be that to you. It just doesn't seem to be God's will—"

With dignity Dovie broke in, "Digby, don't pretend to know what God's will is," and she quoted, "'He is faithful that promised.'"

Sensitive of her grieving heart, Digby said no more. Dulcie, however, pursued the painful subject with her twin.

"Sister, I hate to hurt you, but we're all just so worried. Please let go of this hopeless conviction that God has a child for you—please!"

But Dovie's face was set, and who could disturb the peace, with nothing to substitute for it but hopelessness?

The sad little procession wended its way from the Ivey house, across the yard, into the bush, to the meadow. There—again—a hole waited. There—again—Dovie's dreams were laid.

Dovie herself could not attend. Weeping, pleading, availed nothing. Digby and Anna were steadfast.

"Say your good-byes now, Dovie. You're too weak—

you can't walk it, and you know the buggy can't get through that trail."

That Dovie had chosen such a remote spot as a garden for her babies' beds now worked against her.

"I'll come soon, little one," she whispered. "For now, rest with your brothers. But know this—" Dovie looked around and whispered fiercely (but not so secretly but that Digby didn't hear, and hearing, groaned), "you are the last to rest there!"

Digby was loving and patient; Anna and Dulcie were faithful and encouraging; neighbors offered cheer; the pastor stood—firmly and gently—on his position; and Dovie began to regain her health and to take her place as loving wife, sweet sister, kindly neighbor, and faithful parishioner once again.

But not before Digby had one final talk with his wife. "There are to be no more pregnancies, Dovie."

Dovie looked at him with big eyes and said nothing. Nothing that is, but "Faithful is He that promised."

23

IF BRIDE AND GROOM WERE TO GET ACQUAINTED, it would be in the midst of a heavy work schedule and unrelenting, dawn-to-dark responsibilities.

Hannah awoke to the clank of milk pails. Slipping from bed and into a wrapper that she had unpacked the previous night and hung in the clothes press, she peeked out. The room was empty; her husband had obviously headed for the barn and the milking. But a fire crackled in the range, and a teakettle was beginning to steam.

Slipping out cautiously, Hannah filled the washbasin with warm water, retreated to her room, and proceeded to bathe. The night's rest had eliminated any strain of the journey and the ceremony; youth and good health rebounded, and the face that gazed back at her from the mirror was fresh and bright, showing perhaps a faint flush of color not usually apparent in the creamy pallor of her natural complexion.

And even Hannah's self-critical eye thought she could detect a sparkle in the usually level, usually self-possessed eyes gazing back at her. That this experience might, after all, be something of an adventure had been the least of her expectations. She had been prepared for submission to a galling situation, she had fixed her will to accept a distasteful relationship, she had offered herself (as it were) a lamb on the sacrificial altar of marriage to a man who might

well turn out to be churlish, ignorant, unsympathetic, demanding—and more.

Instead—there had been Matthew and his thoughtful-
ness, his early-morning cheerfulness (she could hear his
whistle even now), with an opportunity to share his
dreams and his hopes—and his home.

Hannah found pleasure in a search of the shelves and
cupboards and in selecting the ingredients for biscuits. She
found herself evaluating the importance of the items she
had brought with her and where they would be disposed
in the house to make it more appealing, more homelike,
more utilitarian.

So engrossed was she in turning out the best scrambled eggs possible that she failed to hear the opening of the
screen, and she started when Matthew's teasing voice said
at her elbow, "Good morning, *wife!*"

Totally unable to respond in kind and boldly call this
stranger "husband," Hannah found herself laughing back
at the grin that made Matthew's term acceptable.

"I'll go ahead and strain the milk," Matthew said,
"and you can see where I keep the pans and straining cloth
and so on."

Hannah watched with part of her attention as she
served the breakfast.

Matthew washed, bending over the basin, and in this
simple movement of his body Hannah was aware of his
beauty. *As beautiful as one of his own thoroughbreds*, she
thought with a pang, remembering her own image in her
mirror earlier and its inadequacies (she felt).

Even when he stood erect, shook the water from his
dark hair, and combed it before the small mirror, revealing
starkly the appalling scar, she knew wonderingly that, for
her, it detracted nothing from the package she accepted as
being Matthew Hunter.

Perhaps her wonder and acceptance spoke wordlessly,
for in that moment Matthew caught sight of her face—

without pretense, or hypocrisy, or evasiveness. But when he turned, eyes alight, Hannah, color a little higher than usual, was pouring coffee.

During the meal—saying yes, she had slept well; yes, she had found what she needed for making breakfast; yes, the day was a beautiful one—Hannah was again aware that Matthew's scrutiny of her face and her expressions far exceeded what was necessary for such a routine conversation. And again she found herself coloring and wished she wouldn't—that *he* wouldn't, for the breathless, high-colored, bright-eyed woman he was conjuring up by his intimate study was a false Hannah! Of that she was certain.

Before he left for the day's work, Matthew suggested he come in early and that Hannah accompany him, once again, to Meridian to get her trunks.

"But it will be in the wagon," he warned, smiling.

"I've ridden in wagons, you know," she responded and wondered why he felt it necessary to make such a statement.

Dressed in her simple percale dress and her sensible shoes, how could she know the percale was "Persian" and even to the untrained eye had a richness all its own? Or that her footwear, which the store termed "common-sense sandals" and assured the buyer were "designed for a thoroughly comfortable house slipper," spoke of quality because of the exceptional grade of "Paris kid" and their handsome cut?

Or that her manners were refined? her speech gracious? her hands well-cared for?

"It will give us an opportunity to talk," Matthew said, "to get acquainted. What a strange thing to need to say to one's bride!" Again the smile, taking the suggestiveness from his words, and bringing a smile in return in spite of herself.

Hannah sorted out her belongings, ironed numerous items, rinsed out the waist she had worn on the trip, and finally tiptoed into the other bedroom to find the bed neatly made, Matthew's clothes put away, his shoes out of sight.

Only the desk was in disarray—or was to her eye. That it was just as Matthew wanted it she was quite sure and refrained from touching any part of it. Scraps of paper were filled with figures; others, in plain sight, contained cryptic references to fetlock . . . poll . . . croup . . . cannons . . . hock . . . and more, obviously all relating to his horses, their purchase, sale, evaluation.

It was on the trip to Meridian that Hannah learned the story of Matthew's injury.

"It was the first thoroughbred I bought," he said ruefully. "I've learned a bit since then—though it could happen again, I suppose.

"It was a very skittish stallion, one that eventually brought me a good return on my investment in stud fees before I sold him. I was riding him—or," with a shake of his head, "trying to. He did nothing but prance, mostly sideways. I had to pull his head around almost to my knee to keep him from running headlong into the barbed wire fence.

"I suppose he wore me out before I wore him out—or I had an unguarded moment when I wasn't in full control. To make a long story short, he threw me. I slid down the barbed wire—clothes torn, some rips to my body here and there—not much. But my face—"

Soberly Matthew told of the barb's chewing into the flesh of his cheek, of somehow getting himself to Anna Snodgrass, of her cleansing of the terrible wound, and sewing, as best she could, the ragged edges together.

"Bad as it was," Matthew finished, "it had its blessings. I've been a better man for it. And now, in its way, it's brought me you. Someday I'll try to explain that to you."

Inexplicably, unexpectedly, Hannah had an impulse to take Matthew's work-hardened hand in hers and simply hold it. It seemed a bold and unacceptable thing to do, and so she refrained. But the impulse had been there! Hannah, pondering this surprising (and suddenly precious) feeling and the warmth it generated in her heart, felt unexpected tears fill her eyes.

Seeing them, Matthew, touched and astonished, reached for her hand, holding it warmly.

And so Hannah had her hand held after all.

Through a wild muddle of feelings (she might have thought more coherently if her hand had not been gripped in Matthew's), Hannah faced the probable truth: She had fallen in love.

Was it possible to love someone you had just met? Knowing it was, Hannah accepted it. Would such a love be enduring, for all time? Knowing it would, Hannah was swept by a sweet wonder. All the restrained ardor, the un-requited love, the unsatisfied cry of her heart, as child and woman, swept from their hiding place and surrendered. All the empty years, the pains of rejection, the undeserved and uncalled-for criticisms washed from her heart in the flood of feeling that captivated her now.

If Matthew thought she turned suddenly speechless, he didn't say. Perhaps he, as she, settled for that comfort-able togetherness that all true love generates. She didn't know—and, not knowing, closed her lids over eyes she felt must surely give her away. Her lips continued to make ap-propriate responses, though curved to laughter and song. Her heart—her staid, controlled heart—danced to a new and lovely tune while she calmly discussed the groceries they would need; loaded her trunks, boxes, and bags; and turned homeward.

That the little log house felt like *home* that evening could have been because her familiar things were strewn around her, her mark set in numerous ways upon its sim-plicity. Hannah didn't try to analyze it; her quick step, her thoughtful placing of a few pictures, her relaxed and graceful movements, all told the story for anyone with eyes to see.

And Matthew watched ceaselessly. Whatever he might be thinking, Hannah—in her happy daze—felt passionately that it must be akin to what she felt.

Nevertheless, at bedtime Matthew said casually, "I have some letters to write—some records to bring up to date. I'll take a lamp and go on in, if you don't mind." And with another searching look before which Hannah's breath stopped and her cheeks flamed, he shut the door to his room.

With the morning, never had the sun shone brighter, never had birds sung sweeter. Even the rooster's crow had a romance to it that made Hannah, wise to her own foolishness, laugh with pleasure as she went about the day's activities.

The rich and exotic merchandise of Vaughn's Royal Emporium faded in importance and significance in comparison with the satisfaction Hannah felt as she disposed her wedding gifts and simple household effects around the house.

Love, she thought with surprise, catching sight of her flushed face, bright eyes, and tumbled hair, *can make you feel beautiful!* Blushing at her foolishness, she reveled in the new sensations she was enjoying.

"Do you like to walk?" Matthew asked at noon when he came in for his dinner. "I thought, if you do, we might walk over to see Gussie and Henry this evening. The evenings are long now, and the walk is pleasant that time of day—"

"I'd love it," Hannah said, watching as Matthew took a jar of water with him and left for an afternoon in the "far field."

Unpacking the pen holder and nibs from her desk at home, and the inkstand with its enamel finish, iron base, and two flint glass bottles, Hannah considered where to put them. The pen holder would make a beautiful addition to Matthew's desk; she would make him a gift of it.

About to set it down, she moved some of the clutter to make room. Arranging the set critically, her glance fell on a portion of a letter that she had exposed—and she stood transfixed.

Without touching the letter—an intrusion of privacy of which she could not be guilty—she read—and reading, died inside:

> . . . sorry to say, she's a disappointment . . . expected something better . . . older too than was represented . . . A good worker no doubt . . . but nothing to look at! . . . too late now . . . make the best of a bad bargain. . . .

Cheeks as white as the paper at which she stared, Hannah felt her world tip and spin and finally whirl her off into a blankness where pain was not allowed, nor anger, nor questioning—and hardly any sanity.

With stiff fingers she packed a few things in her bag. Thank goodness, she thought foolishly, she had washed her waist—what better outfit to leave in than the one in which she came? Thank goodness she had had the good sense to slip some money into her purse (had she subconsciously expected rejection?), enough money to see her back to safety and to sanity.

The afternoon was early; Matthew would be gone for several hours. An hour—less—to get to Gussie's. A little longer to get to the station, and it would all be just a memory, another memory to shut the door on, another memory too painful for remembering.

Pitiful as it was, perhaps, she had her pride. Seating herself at the table, she wrote: *"Matthew: It won't work. I'll fit better back where I came from. Don't ask me to come back. Good-bye. Hannah."*

After that, it only remained to prop it in plain sight, put on her hat and gloves, pick up her bag, shut the door, and leave.

Gussie went from horrified gasps to helpless despair, only to capitulate to her friend's unyielding request. Henry took a quiet Hannah to the station, left her there to await the train, and went home to face a white-faced Matthew.

"I thought," he managed before he turned back to his empty house, "she was—for real. She certainly had me fooled."

"If you could tell me what happened, Matthew—," Gussie begged.

"That's just it, Gussie. I don't know. She just—changed her mind, I guess."

"You don't know Hannah, Matthew! If I could just tell you about her life—what has made her the person she is—"

"Some other time," Matthew said tiredly. "If it matters any longer."

Dawn found Hannah free of the bush and its memories. The endless expanse of the prairie seemed no more unending than the future that stretched before her, empty and bleak. So bleak.

24

"ARE THESE WHEELS WELL-IRONED AND BOILED in hot oil?" Holly asked through chattering teeth as the wagon jounced and bounced over the prairie.

"Ironed? Boiled in hot oil?" Uncle Syl asked blankly.

"High-class wagons have this feature," Holly said, her wisdom a result of many long, lonely hours spent with the catalog.

"They do, eh? All I know," and Uncle Syl pushed his old hat back and scratched his head, driving with one hand, "is that the wheels go around like they should. And, of course, I'm mighty pleased with this spring seat."

And Uncle Syl jounced and bounced experimentally. Holly, on the other end of the seat, hung onto the armrest tightly during the undulation of her perch; Neddy, in the middle, laughed and bounced happily. It was good to be out of the sound of Aunt Elsie's voice and away from her sharp eyes.

"How far have we got to go?" Neddy asked, hoping it would be miles and miles.

"Miles and miles," Uncle Syl answered and stirred the plodding horses to a faster gait. "But we'll have time to fill the barrels and gather a lot of wood before dark. We'll finish the job in the morning, get on our way, and be home before chore time tomorrow."

On the floor bed, their cooking supplies clattered and

their drinking water sloshed. Holly cast a speculative eye toward her bag, checking again in her mind the items she had included for the great adventure ahead.

Besides the loaded bag, there would be their jackets to carry and their bedding—two of Mama's handmade quilts. When Uncle Syl had thrown in a tarpaulin, "just in case," Holly had added her father's black oiled cover. Six by eight feet in size, it would fold neatly, and Neddy could carry it; she had a feeling they would be glad they had it along—for storms or night's dews. Scrupulously honest, she wouldn't consider taking one that belonged to the Crabbes, though Uncle Syl said, "Take mine, then, if you think you have to have one."

Holly's insistence, in this as in other items (such as bringing her father's hatchet), had caused Elsie to roll her eyes at her husband and say, "I declare—I never saw such a strong-minded child!"

The wagon loaded, Uncle Syl and Neddy in place, Holly had delayed the departure by one last dash into the house. With Aunt Elsie fussing around the wagon, Holly felt free, now, to slip her note out of her pocket, lay it on the dresser, and add a postscript: "The money is to pay for the food we're taking with us."

And she had laid some coins beside the note, grateful again for those she had found in her parents' clothing.

Climbing into the wagon, she had said quickly, "I'm ready, Uncle Syl."

"Wagons ho!" Neddy had shouted, and in the hustle and bustle of settling down, waving, and getting the lurching rig underway, Holly had watched anxiously until they were out of sight. Only then did she relax, knowing Aunt Elsie had no way of pursuing them. Holly wasn't sure Aunt Elsie would want to.

In spite of the increasing heat and the continuous rough motion, the morning passed pleasantly. *Northward—ever northward*, sang the childish heart of the little girl. With

every thud of the horses' hooves, every creak of the com-
plaining wagon, the faint thin line of green drew nearer.
Noontime found them seated under one of the scattered
bushes now dotting the landscape, eating the lunch Aunt
Elsie had packed for them. The milk was warm. And
creamy enough, Uncle Syl said, so that they would have
butter before the day was over, what with the jiggling of
the wagon!

In spite of the motion, or perhaps because of it, Neddy
grew drowsy when they resumed the trip and was soon
asleep in the bottom of the rig, missing the coolness of the
atmosphere as the trees and bush increased. He awoke
when, with a jolt, the wagon tumbled down the incline into the steep-walled ravine that was the coulee. Leaning his
arms on the wagon side, he watched, entranced, as the
green closed around them and they pushed their way
along a well-traveled trail to a wide spot.

"Whoa, girls!" Uncle Syl pulled the rig to a halt.

Neddy and Holly were over the side and running for
the water almost before the wheels had stopped turning.
Pulling off their shoes and stockings, they waded in, splash-
ing and shrieking and, in general, having a hilarious time.

Eventually Uncle Syl called, reminding them that they
had come along, after all, to help.

Holly was well familiar with pitching camp. Her set
little face might have revealed to a more sensitive observer
than Syl Crabbe that the entire process was filled with
memories—with voices and smiles and hugs—

"Neddy—," she said unsteadily and dropped her
work and stepped aside to take her brother in her arms in
a fierce hug. He, in turn—little more than a baby and much
in need of a mother's arms—clung to his sister, his small
arms going around her thin form and his curly head pressing against her waist.

"I don't want to go back, Sissy," he whispered. "Can't
we stay here—in the cool?"

"We'll see, Neddy," Holly said quietly, not daring to say more.

"Uncle Syl could stay, if he wanted to, but not Aunt Elsie!" And Neddy shook his red-gold curls decisively.

"Let's help Uncle Syl now," Holly suggested, and the children spent the rest of the afternoon searching out fallen wood, helping dip water, and later, getting supper. Uncle Syl opened a jar of chicken while Holly fried potatoes over the campfire, finishing off with a piece of Aunt Elsie's one-egg cake and a cup of tea, weakened down, in Neddy's case, with a generous lacing of milk. (The milk, not yet butter as Uncle Syl had supposed, had been quickly placed in the stream.)

When the stars came out one by one, Holly tucked Neddy into a bed of quilts. Uncle Syl pulled off his boots and sat musing by the fire until he too sought his blankets.

"I'll sit up a little longer, Uncle Syl," Holly said, "and I'll make sure the fire is out before I—before I leave it."

Though she was tired from the day's ride and activities, sleep was no threat; she and Neddy would slip away just as soon as she was sure Uncle Syl was asleep, giving a longer time to travel before their absence was discovered. Tensely she waited.

The worst time was just ahead. If they were to be found out now—and stopped—Holly shivered at the fireside and listened to the distant, regular snore.

When the long evening had turned to the blackness of night, Holly doused the fire. Listening, she was relieved to find that the noise had not roused the sleeping man. Uncle Syl was apparently a heavy sleeper.

Before she woke Neddy, she assembled her equipment—the bag, oiled cover, their coats, and awkwardly, the hatchet tied around her waist with a rope.

Uncle Syl slept.

Creeping to Neddy's side, Holly roused him.

"Neddy," she breathed into his ear, "Neddy! Wake up!"

Neddy came awake to find his sister's hand over his mouth. "Listen carefully, Neddy. We're going to go find Mama's—Mama's—" Holly didn't know the relationship of the man whose name was in her mother's Bible. "Mama's cousin. But we have to do it quietly—Uncle Syl mustn't know.

"Now—get up—that's it—very quietly." Holly kept urging the small boy with whispers and guiding him with her hands—into his shoes, into his coat (easier to wear than carry, at this point).

Something stirred and the children crouched, hardly breathing, until they determined it was the stamping of a horse. Then she folded Neddy's quilts as snugly as possible, tied them together with another length of rope, and hoisted the rope to her shoulder. She thrust the oiled cover into Neddy's arms, picked up her bag, and whispered, "I can't hold your hand, Neddy. You'll have to hold onto me."

With Neddy clutching her skirt, Holly turned toward the escarpment.

Her decision had been made: they would follow the road.

Although the coulee beckoned, with its thick brush and cool water, Holly wasn't sure where it went. And even if they just hid in it until Syl had gone, they would waste considerable time, perhaps a full day. Considering their small food supply and the distance they had to go, Holly figured they should be on their way and quickly.

And so from just before midnight—the time of true dark this time of year—until the moment the sky began to lighten in the east, a short night indeed, the children trudged the well-beaten track. But not back the way they had come; Holly had watched carefully and knew where the turning was and found it readily in the faint light cast by a half-moon.

Occasionally they stopped for rest; once Neddy's head

drooped and Holly let him sleep for a few minutes. Then she urged him on.

Although the whole escapade was news to Neddy, he didn't question the rightness of it nor Holly's wisdom in making the decision. And didn't it mean the last of "Aunt" Elsie? Holly had only to suggest that Uncle Syl might find them and take them back, to give Neddy's lagging feet renewed energy.

With dawn came a view of the interminable prairie with its endless vistas of grass. As far as the eye could see, the seemingly limitless plain stretched, but ever more and more behind them as their steps led north—always north.

And more and more the taller growth appeared, at first scattered, but always beckoning—beckoning north.

When far back down the road Holly thought she saw the first puff of dust that might mean a rig, she veered from the road into the growth and grass.

"We'll stop here for a while, Neddy," she said, studying the density of the growth, the distance they had come from the road, and the shade available. Neddy sank down with a sigh, his face white beneath a coating of dust.

Laying the oiled cover under the edge of a bushy patch, the children sat down. From her bag Holly produced a loaf of bread, a small bottle of water, and her father's knife. Hacking off a couple of chunks, they ate and drank and laid their weary heads back and went to sleep.

It was a rough boot in her side that woke her.

"Well, lookee here! Two little runaways, or my name ain't Mordecai Clinch!"

WITH SMALL HANKY PLAYING ON THE RUG WITH Beggar, Gussie paced the floor, shooting dark looks at the white face of the man sitting stiffly and silently in the straight chair in the house that still bore traces of Hannah's presence.

"What in heaven's name happened?" Gussie, in dismay and despair, threw caution to the winds and asked the question bluntly.

"I wish I knew." Matthew's voice was toneless. But his jaws worked with tension, and the ragged scar stood out in white relief against his bronzed cheek.

"You must have done something!" Gussie said wrathfully. "If you hurt Hannah—" Her small foot stamped alarmingly.

Such a thunderous glance shot from Matthew's dark eyes that even Gussie faltered.

"Well then—," Gussie floundered.

"You're the one who knows her," Matthew said. "I'm at a loss to explain it. She seemed—she seemed—" He paused, remembering that last evening.

He remembered the softening of Hannah's face, the spring in her step, the open, almost breathtaking glimpse of her heart, a heart making an innocent offer, a tentative offer. Knowing her so briefly, he hadn't been sure. But his glimpse of it and the possibilities it promised had caused his heart to leap. There was hope for them!

What a dolt he had been! Why hadn't he followed up the sweet opportunity!

"I thought there was a chance for us," he said finally. "Then I was almost immediately uncertain, and I was so afraid of rushing in—of taking advantage. It was a mistake, I guess," Matthew spoke despairingly. "Not knowing, eager but hesitant, afraid to hope and yet hoping, I went to, well, to my room—"

Gussie looked thoughtful.

"—filled with a wild sort of joy, Gussie. It was going to be all right! I walked the floor, just sort of rejoicing that things would, after all, turn out right; and praying, asking for wisdom on how to proceed sensitively. Next morning, Hannah was sparkling—"

Hannah, sparkling? The whole thing was confusing to Gussie.

"I went to work confident she was feeling as good about things as I was. I came back—to find her gone." Matthew's voice shook.

"Do you think she might have felt rejected?" Gussie asked frankly.

"Rejected? So little was said, by either of us, Gussie; surely she understood my hesitation—my uncertainties—"

"Let me tell you about Hannah, Matthew," Gussie said and proceeded to explain the facts of Hannah's loveless childhood, her repeated rejection by a father she adored, and her conviction, finally, that it was because of her personal liabilities and lack.

One thing Gussie held back—she made no reference to Morris Vaughn's wealth or that Hannah had inherited it. Knowing Matthew, Gussie was certain he would never lift a finger to bring her back if he knew.

"So you see," Gussie said, finishing the sad story, "she really didn't expect love to be any part of this marriage. That's why she agreed to this—this cold-blooded arrangement and was willing to settle for it.

"But she's not so different from you, Matthew! You, too, have a great need—oh, you thought it was hidden!—to have someone love you just for yourself. If not love, then acceptance, just because you're you!"

"So," Matthew said heavily, "she thought she was rejected. But to leave so precipitately! She gave me no chance!"

"You'll write her, Matthew? Beg her to come back?" Gussie's voice was anxious.

"She asked me not to, Gussie. A man has his pride, you know." Matthew's voice firmed, and he continued, "I'll carry on as I have been. But her things—will you take care of them, Gussie?"

Gussie nodded, wiping her eyes.

"I'll get her trunks and boxes."

Gussie gave Hanky a crust to chew on and went about the dreary task of folding Hannah's clothes and packing them away, removing the household articles she had set in places of her choice and packing them.

"Do you see anything I've missed?" she asked, finally.

"You got it all, I think. Except for a pen holder and some writing material she put on my desk."

Reaching for the handsome set of bottles and pens, Gussie's eyes fell on a half-exposed letter: ". . . she's a disappointment . . . expected something better . . . older too than was represented . . . nothing to look at . . . best of a bad bargain . . ."

Gussie put her hands over her face as waves of pain and anger almost made her reel.

Finally, "Matthew!" she managed in a terrible voice.

"Yes? What is it?" Matthew entered the room, strode to Gussie's side.

Wordless, white of face, shaken beyond words, Gussie pointed a trembling finger toward the letter and its cruel evaluation: *disappointment . . . older . . . bad bargain . . .*

26

"HOW MUCH LONGER, SISTER, DO YOU SUPPOSE we'll have to do the work of two households?"

A musical tinkle accompanied Dulcie's question as the peas she was shelling fell from her hands into the kettle on her lap.

"As long as it's needed." As always, Anna was brisk and forthright. "And we can manage, busy as we are, with Shaver to take on so many of the responsibilities at home."

"Yes, God bless him—what would we do without him? I'm not reluctant to do Dovie's work, Sister," Dulcie said, with a cautious glance toward the open door, "but I'm just so anxious for her to begin to feel like herself again."

"It will take time, Sister."

Dulcie sighed. "It's not only her poor little worn-out body, Anna—"

"I know. It's her poor little worn-out mind."

"Anna! What a thing to say!"

"Well, does she seem entirely rational to you? Half the time she's crying over the loss of her baby; the other half she's spouting that—that—"

"Promise."

"Promise indeed! She'd be healthier, all told, if she could be persuaded to stop being so stubborn about something that obviously can't come true. Digby says—"

"I know what Digby says. But Dovie can be mighty

persuasive. And he loves her very much. And she wants another baby very badly."

"It's her *life* we're talking about now, Dulcie! Digby won't take a chance on losing her. No, I think you may count out any cooperation from Digby."

"Can't that pastor of ours," Dulcie said grimly and all unfairly, "get across to her how *wrong*, how very *wrong* it is of her not to be more submissive to God's will?"

*   *   *

"I've never felt more helpless in my life," the pastor said.

"You've explained about that scripture of hers being the words of Jesus about himself, I'm sure," Ellie said thoughtfully.

"And do you know her answer? She quotes Isaiah 55 where it says about the rain and the snow coming down: 'so shall my word be,' Dovie quotes. 'It shall accomplish that which I please.'"

"How can you answer arguments like that?"

"I don't know that I should, Ellie. I can't bring myself to destroy that gleam of hope in Dovie's white little face. I'm just not able to be that harsh."

"Maybe in time as she heals she can accept this blow. It's bad to lose one's baby—it's shattering, I should think, to feel betrayed by the Lord."

"Yes—in time; that's my hope. Eventually Dovie will be able to face the baby's death and believe that God has, after all, been with her throughout it all. In the meantime, we'll continue to love her and stand by her as she clings like the proverbial limpet to scripture she interprets as a promise."

"And Digby? Surely he requires the wisdom of Solomon and the patience of Job in all of this."

*   *   *

Holding the precious little person of his wife to him and living again those frightening hours when her life hung in the balance, feeling her loving arms creep around his neck and hearing her persuasive murmurs, Digby could only groan inwardly and stiffen his resistance to Dovie's ever-so-reasonably presented arguments and stand by his decision.

"You see, Digby, it's *bound* to go well next time. 'God, that cannot lie, promised.'"

It was so unfair of her to use scripture as a tool against him! In happier, saner times she would have known it. Now Digby could only grit his teeth in silent frustration and gently maintain his position.

Once, once only did he grow stern, even sharp, in his helplessness and frustration.

"There will be no more babies, Dovie! Let us grieve decently for little Charles, please! Let us not offer up our sorrow over his loss on the spurious altar to another, unborn, child!"

Only when he saw Dovie's already pale face whiten still more and watched the silent running of her tears did Digby grasp the depths of her pain and the unswerving fight for the faith that would overcome.

"Lovie—Lovie—," Digby groaned, as broken as she but without the consolation.

It took all the manhood he had to look into those hope-lit eyes when Dovie whispered one last agonized, "*Please*—" and repeat once and for all time: "No."

"Then," said Dovie quietly, "He'll just have to find another way, won't He? And that will be even more of a miracle, won't it?"

✳ ✳ ✳

Tears fell like rain that summer in Wildrose. Heartbroken for her two friends, Hannah and Dovie, Gussie wept often and copiously. Only Hanky's anxious face stemmed the tide and dried her eyes.

Hugging the little one to her, Gussie counted her

blessings: a loving husband (unlike Hannah), a precious baby (unlike Dovie), and, again unlike poor Dovie, the promise of another new life. Gussie held one child against the other—the seen and the unseen—and treasured her health and her happiness as never before.

Of all the family and friends, Gussie was probably the only one who stood with Dovie in her fixation concerning the promise of a child.

"It makes sense to me," she said stoutly to Henry. "After all, does it sound sensible to be told to go bathe in the river Jordan and your cancer will be healed? And Peter—walking on the water! That *Jesus* could and did—that makes sense, everyone agrees. But for *Peter* to step out and do it—foolishness!"

"Yes, and Peter nearly drowned, as I remember," Henry reminded his wife mildly.

"But that wasn't the Lord's fault! Peter *doubted*. And down he went! Dovie is holding on as if her very life depends on it. And maybe it does!"

"Back off, Sweetie!" Henry said, laughing. "No need to get ferocious with *me!*"

"Well—it just makes me—makes me—" And Gussie teared up again and could only be consoled in Henry's arms.

"As if that weren't enough," she sniffed, drying her eyes, "there's this situation with Hannah! How I wish she'd write!"

"Give her time, Honey."

"I can just picture her—back in her lonely house, facing the questions in all those eyes. Taking up her old routine at the store. Oh!" And Gussie sobbed afresh and was comforted afresh.

27

HEE, HEE, HEE! TWO LITTLE BUSH MICE! HAD YOUR nest discovered, din't ya?" And the boot nudged her again.

Gasping, Holly sat up, staring up at the unsavory face of the stranger.

The narrow eyes were lit with a wicked glee; the damp mouth grinned to display broken teeth surrounded by a straggly graying beard in a gaunt face.

"Think a blind person couldn't foller them tracks of yers? Saw where they turned off, plain as the nose on yer face." And the dirty paw tweaked Holly Carroll's nose before she could turn her horrified face aside.

Neddy, awake and afraid, set up a wail. "Leave my sister alone!"

The grinning face scowled, and the grimy paw turned mean. Grabbing Neddy's arm, the man snatched him out of his bed of quilts and shook him, as a terrier might a gopher. When he let the child go, Neddy sank into his sister's ready arms—ready, because she had them fixed for a furious flailing of the interloper.

"Git yer things together—quick," the stranger commanded. "C'mon!" And he booted Neddy in the rear when the little boy picked blindly at their belongings.

Holly quickly put the oiled cover into Neddy's arms, folded the blankets, and tried to tie them.

"Gimme those!" Mordecai Clinch snatched impatiently at the bundle, tucked it under one arm, and yanked Holly to her feet with the other.

With her bag trailing through the grasses and bush around her, Holly was trundled roughly toward the road, Neddy following willy-nilly.

"You came from thataway—"

The man squinted southward. "But I ain't goin' thataway! Too bad fer yer folks—or whosomever you was runnin' from. If they come lookin', they kin have ye, but fer a price!" And a cackle issued from the pink lips.

"And if they don't come—and somethin' tells me they won't—I'll just have an instant family. How about that! A boy," Mordecai looked with some disfavor on the white-faced Neddy, "and," eyes brightening, "a girl!"

And Mordecai's next tweak was more painfully (and more personally) delivered than the first had been.

Enraged, Neddy delivered a hefty kick to the man's skinny shin.

"Yow! Why, you little—" Cursing, Mordecai Clinch swatted the little boy such a blow that it sent him sprawling in the road, to mingle his tears with the dust.

Hopping painfully, the man grunted, "Now git yerselves up into that there buggy, you little varmints!"

When Holly showed signs of refusing, Mordecai threatened, "Git up there or I'll leave the *baby* behind." And Holly helped her brother to his feet and herded him toward an ancient buggy and single horse.

"Up with ye!" To avoid the man's hands, Holly climbed up quickly, set down her bulky bag, and reached for Neddy's hand.

"Now set down and be still whilst I stow these here quilts away. Purty, ain't they?"

Walking around the wheel, the man turned toward the box-like back of the body, behind the seat. Shoving aside his own gear, he made a place for the quilts.

Dazed, numb, scarcely aware of the terrible thing that had happened to them, Holly acted on an impulse born of desperation.

Staring hopelessly around for any sign of human help, her eyes lit on the buggy whip. Pushing Neddy back into the seat, she snatched the whip from its socket, drew her arm back in a wide arc, and with a snap that rang on the air like the crackle of lightning, lashed the broad back of the horse.

Startled, hurt, alarmed, the animal leaped, throwing Neddy painfully against the seat back, almost overthrowing Holly, and jerking the buggy from the hand of the man.

The second blow and Holly's screamed "Giddap!" sent the horse plunging into the harness, whinnying in fear, and charging down the road, mane streaming, legs a-gallop, hooves pounding, clods of dirt flying.

Neddy hung on for dear life; Holly rode the bucketing rig like a sailor rides the tossing sea, engaged now in handling the reins, having tossed the whip aside.

Mordecai Clinch, having tried desperately to get a grip on the back of the buggy and failing, found himself, after a hundred or so yards of futile running, far outdistanced and hopelessly outrun. If Holly had dared take her eyes from the horse to look back, she would have seen the dust rising round the feet of the man who danced in impotent rage, shaking his fist, dashing his hat to the ground, and trampling it. If she had been able to hear above the buggy's racketing convulsions, Neddy's squeals, and the animal's wild blowing and snorting, she would have heard the curses and bitter threats Mordecai Clinch shrieked, with spittle flying and teeth gnashing.

Miles down the road—a road mercifully free of traffic—with the horse blown and yielding readily now to Holly's steady drag on the reins, she pulled it to a trembling halt, its head tossing and its eyes rolling.

Holly, shaking from fear and from the physical energy

expended, sank down into the buggy seat at last and considered their options as the horse settled down, its sides slowed their heaving, and its head dropped wearily.

"This isn't our rig," she explained to Neddy. "I suppose I should turn it around and start it back down the road while we try to hide."

Neddy's eyes filled with apprehension.

"Or," Holly said thoughtfully, "we could just borrow this rig for a while, and go on."

Neddy's sigh of relief and urgent nods confirmed her suggestion and firmed it into resolution.

Now, at last, she looked back. Not knowing how far they'd come, she knew it was several miles and there was little chance of seeing the brutal man who had precipitated the entire scenario. But there was always the possibility that he would catch a ride with a passing rig.

Gently now, she clucked to the horse and urged the outfit forward, grateful that Mordecai Clinch had been headed north and they were miles closer to their destination.

Now the bush not only beckoned but welcomed them. The farmhouses were built near the road rather than back down a dusty road in the middle of a prairie section. Passing first one, then two, and eventually a third and fourth, Holly began to relax when she realized their passing was no different than that of a dozen other rigs that might go by in a day. A few people waved, some called a cheery greeting.

Finally, Holly turned the horse into a nearby yard where a woman was drawing water.

"May we water our horse?" Holly asked politely, and the homesteader gladly gave permission.

"Have some yourselves," she invited, and Holly and Neddy descended, drank thirstily from the edge of the woman's fresh-drawn pail, and turned to go.

"Come far?" the stranger asked compassionately.

"Yes," Holly admitted cautiously.

"You're welcome to rest a bit," the woman said, her eyes sympathetic. "Come on in—"

When Holly refused, politely, the woman urged the children to sit on the steps, "at least," and she brought out glasses of milk and a plate of sweet-buttered bread. Holly and Neddy ate hungrily—and thankfully.

"Thank you," Holly said and hesitantly started to withdraw the small coin purse from her pocket, putting it back quickly when the woman's eyes flashed and she said, "No—please. It's the way we do things here. You'll have a chance to do the same someday."

Humbly, blushing at her near-insult, Holly stumblingly expressed her thanks again, helped Neddy up into the buggy, turned the refreshed horse, and went on her way.

"People are good here, Neddy," she said. "There are more good people than bad—remember that."

But Neddy, his memories still vivid, looked back fearfully.

As the day waned, Holly pulled the rig off the road into a stand of birches surrounded by bush, but only out of pity for the horse. She would have driven all night, or until darkness made it impossible, with Neddy's head on her lap.

Uncertain about the hitching process, Holly left the horse in harness, tied to a tree. But she and Neddy gathered armfuls of sweet grass and piled it before the weary animal.

"I'm still hungry, Sissy," Neddy said plaintively.

Opening her bag, Holly studied its contents: bread for a few days, some canned goods, a piece of drying cheese.

She held up a can of peas and sighed: no opener. Fortunately, Da's hatchet was still at her waist.

"Stand back, Neddy," she said and gave the can a mighty thwack. Juice ran from the split can, but the children salvaged most of the peas.

For the first time Holly realized Mama's quilts were in the buggy. Feeling a sense of comfort from the familiar, loved items, she and Neddy wrapped themselves up, found a grassy spot, and were soon asleep.

With the first dazzling light of morning winking at them through the leaves, they were up, had eaten some bread and cheese, had had a drink from a nearby stream, and were on their way.

Mostly plodding, sometimes trotting, the horse took them through ever-deepening bush, past rough farms with their small fields, a struggling town.

And so the days passed in a round of simple meals, a refreshing bath in an isolated slough (and a quivering, shuddering pulling-off of leeches), several stops at wells and friendly farmhouses, and numerous inquiries.

"Wildrose? Never heard of it. Meridian? That's a hamlet on ahead of you. Just keep on—"

North, always north.

"Wildrose? That's a *district*, not a town. Lots of districts roundabout, very few towns. Meridian will be your post office. When you get there, it's just a hop, skip, and a jump to Wildrose."

At several homes Holly was able to persuade a cashpoor farmer's wife to part with eggs and bread and milk, once some fresh-baked cookies, and another time a jar of freshly simmered stew, paying for the items gladly from her small store.

Never again did they meet a "bad man," to Neddy's relief and Holly's appreciation. There were more people willing to help than those bent on hindering; it was a country of "God's people" for sure!

But what would she find at Wildrose? What would this—Holly pulled out her mother's Bible and the slip of paper that had wooed them all the way from Ontario, with its nebulously identified stranger—this Gerald Victor—what would he be like?

With childhood's blind faith, Holly's innate stubbornness, and driven by the sheer desperation of their situation, the children pressed on, through heat, dust, a few rain showers, weary days, and aching bodies—for a place called Wildrose.

# 28

HANNAH STOOD HELPLESSLY AND IMPOTENTLY in her old office. Wanting to help, needing to keep busy, there seemed no place for her.

Karl was very kind. "We'll move Peter out," he offered, "and you can move right back in."

But Peter clearly had things under control, even in so short a time. Even more, he was enjoying himself as assistant to his father.

"Not at all!" Hannah protested. "I'm—I'm going back to the house soon. I'll just walk through the store, look around, get the feel of things again—"

Karl watched, puzzled and uneasy, as Hannah left the office area. She had made no explanation except to say, crisply and briefly, "I'm back, and here I'll be, as though I hadn't been gone, Karl."

But Karl wasn't the only one to doubt that life could ever be the same for Hannah again.

Aimlessly wandering the aisles of the store, nodding casually to clerk and customer alike, it seemed to Hannah a dream trip far removed from the reality of life.

The millinery department, with its "Bon Ton," sure to be "much seen on the boulevards of fine cities this summer"; the "Suzanne," a "triumph of millinery art"; the plumes of ostrich tips; the mourning sprays; the wax- and orange-blossom bridal wreaths—all, all so pointless, so frivolous.

The expensive gewgaws at the novelty counter seemed from another world, *for* another world: solid sterling silver handkerchief holder, "with pin on back to attach to dress"; the baby rattle, a heavy solid pearl ring with two solid sterling silver bells; the sterling silver button hook; the silk satin garter with solid silver mountings "very fancy with raised ornamentation"; the solid silver-mounted hose darner, whose "handle is detachable and has a receptacle on the inside for needles"—all, all seemed so unreal, even ridiculous against the background of log houses, Fels Naptha soap, and stove pokers.

Quickly, as though impatient with the fripperies of life, Hannah turned with relief to the uninspired display of common household necessities. "Pudding pan—extra deep"— she hadn't seen one of those in Matthew's kitchen. "Lemonade shaker"—she scorned it! sturdy but pretty japanned bread box—Matthew's was battered; a long-handled corn popper—what a special item to have! Why hadn't she thought to take that when she went? She could almost see it hanging on Matthew's wall and feel the pleasure it would provide on a long winter evening.

Finally, among the countless purchases available— pepper box, clothes sprinkler, tea steeper, radish grater, wire broiler, gravy strainer, patty pan, and flat-iron heater—one small item caught Hannah's eye.

Three inches by one inch it was, and her heart yearned for it. Three cents it cost, but she would have paid any amount.

With something that sounded strangely like a sob and with what seemed disturbingly like tears raining down her pale cheeks, Hannah picked up the biscuit cutter.

If only she'd had a biscuit cutter!

Somehow all the pain, all the anguish centered on the small scrap of tin and its absence in that other life, in another time. All unreasonably, the lack of a biscuit cutter broke her heart.

Never counting it foolish, and forgetting her rule never to take anything, unpaid, from the store, Hannah clutched the small scrap of tin to her breast and blinded by tears and unaware of them, she brushed past a startled clerk, stumbled through the aisles, out onto the street and home.

Hours later she arose from her bed, exhausted, drained of emotion and empty of dreams, and walked deliberately to her dresser. Removing a velvet-lined box, she lifted the lid and gently laid the biscuit cutter among her mother's rich assortment of rings, pendants, necklaces, and brooches.

The lid, when she closed it, snapped with a hollow finality, and Hannah slid the box into the drawer and shut it. About to turn away, she was arrested by her reflection in the mirror over the dresser. Eyes puffed, face pale, hair in disarray, collar crushed, it was Hannah at her worst. Shrinking from it, she almost fancied she could see the shadowy face of her father at her shoulder, mouthing his stinging "ordinary!"

Hearing the contemptuous indictment of her earthly father with her human ear, her spirit—astonishingly, surely—heard the loving whisper of her Heavenly Father: *"Thou wast precious in my sight."*

The scrap of scripture, learned at some earlier day through a faithful Sunday School teacher (who also emphasized, "Thy word have I hid in mine heart"), rang in Hannah's bruised spirit, ushering in a new day as surely as birdsong whistles up the dawn.

Her Heavenly Father loved her. How softly, how sweetly the realization touched, clung, and fixed itself in Hannah's heart!

Overcome by the wonder of it, Hannah turned swiftly to the side of her bed, dropped to her knees, and lost herself in the other-worldly fellowship of the "Father of mercies, and the God of all comfort."

There followed an hour so precious, so personal, so

healing that the time slipped away as a few minutes might in the presence of one's dearest love. And from that hour she arose able, for the first time, to receive love—and though she couldn't know it yet—to give love.

Bathing her face and straightening her hair, Hannah leaned toward the mirror and saw herself "accepted in the beloved." Hannah—just—just *plain accepted!*

Fresh tears mingled with laughter, to be interrupted by a knock at the door of her room and Tilda's low voice:

"Miss Hannah! There's someone to see you. He says—he says his name is Matthew Hunter."

29

WHEN THE SMALL HAMLET APPEARED THROUGH the bush—general store, post office, smithy, railway station, several small houses, and a towering granary—Holly could hardly believe it. Meridian! At long last!

Behind the weary travelers were several towns much like it. Fading from memory were the suspicious questions along the way, the curious looks, the kind offers of help, the free meals, the warnings, the suggestions, the farmer who fixed a broken tug, the woman who washed their bedraggled clothes . . .

"There's a Mountie patrolling around here right now," the same woman had said casually. "If I had any reason to lay low for a while—"

And Holly had laid low, proceeding finally with caution. And the road, always and ever, led north.

"You're heading toward Prince Albert," she was reassured from time to time. "You'll come across Meridian before you get that far. Can't miss it if you just stay on this road."

Worse than the weariness, their sunburn, their general shagginess, was Holly's worry over Neddy's condition. Neddy's chubby little arms and legs seemed match-stick for size; his color was pale under the burn, his eyes listless. Frightened, Holly could only press on.

She knew they had reached Meridian because the

name was printed on the elevator. Climbing down from the buggy, she and a drooping Neddy went into the store.

"Hello, Mister," Holly said politely.

"Why, hello there, stranger. What can I do for you?" Among so many newcomers, many of them hardly able to speak English, most of them desperately poor, Holly's appearance was no different from that of dozens of others who passed by.

Holly unfolded the scrap of paper she had removed from her mother's Bible.

"Do you know this man?" she asked.

"Gerald Victor. Sure do. He's the preacher at Wildrose. Lives out here about, oh, I'd say about five miles."

Holly's relief was so great she felt a moment's giddiness.

"Say, Missy—you feeling all right?"

"I'm fine. What road goes to Wildrose, Mister?"

"Just cross the tracks, Missy," and the man's finger pointed the way. "Rev. Victor expectin' you? Your folks outside?"

Holly was adept at turning questions aside. "We're awful thirsty, Mister," she said.

"I have milk, of course, or Wild Cherry Phosphate." The proprietor seemed particularly proud of this last suggestion. "We buy it in bulk—15 cents per gallon—and we make up our own. It's not cold, of course. I can let you have a glass for," the man hesitated, looking down at the tired face of the girl and the pale face of the boy, "two cents. Water's free."

"We'll take the water, please."

The children drank thirstily. "Might as well take a few crackers from the barrel," the man suggested and felt richly repaid by the smile Holly flashed him and the eager way she reached for the proffered food, selecting, with restraint, four only.

"I declare, Gordon," his wife said as the children filed

out of the building, "you'll run us into the poorhouse if you keep giving free crackers to every Tom, Dick, and Heinrich who comes through the—" Her voice faded as Holly came through the door one more time.

"Mister," Holly asked humbly, "have you got a piece of paper I could write a note on?"

"Will this do?" The store owner tore open an old envelope and handed it to her. "Ah—need a pencil?"

Leaning on the counter, Holly thoughtfully printed a few words: PROPERTY OF MORDEKIE CLENCH.

At the edge of town Holly drew the rig to a halt, and she and Neddy climbed down and unloaded their gear. Locating a rock, she placed the note on the buggy seat and anchored it in place with the rock. Stepping back from the rig she gave a sharp command to the weary horse, whacked it on its rump, and ran alongside until she had the entire contraption headed, driverless, south.

Just five miles from her destination, caution had told her she dared not have the rig and horse found in Wildrose, should the Mounties come looking. Moreover, bad though Mordecai Clinch was, she couldn't rob him.

She did the best she could; her childish conscience felt a great load lift from it when the horse and buggy turned back.

"Come, Neddy," she said, shouldering her much-lighter bag and thrusting—for the last time, she hoped—the oiled cover into Neddy's arms. "We're almost there. P'haps we'll be there by suppertime."

But it was not to be. Neddy grew wearier until he seemed to stagger. Sitting down to rest, Holly felt his brow—it was burning hot.

"P'haps we'll have to stop one more night," she muttered, half to herself, half to the boy whose too-bright eyes and too-red cheeks and drooping shoulders frightened her.

Catching a brief glimpse of a horse and rider over the brow of a small rise in the road behind them, Holly was sure there was a flash of red. A Mountie!

Catching up their belongings and dragging her brother, Holly scrambled through the bush. Pulling Neddy down beside her, they lay quietly hidden until the sound of the rider—a farmer in a faded red shirt—clopped into silence.

To be caught now and turned back, given over to Mordecai Clinch or even to Aunt Elsie and Uncle Syl, was unthinkable.

"We'll stay off the road," Holly decided, and though it made for difficult passage, they thrashed their way through the underbrush at times, crossed plowed fields at times, bypassed a couple of farm yards too close to Meridian to be in Wildrose.

The sun was sinking when Neddy, with a sigh, tumbled in a silent little heap. Encouragement failed to rouse him; gentle shaking availed nothing.

"I can't leave him and go on," Holly thought despairingly. "I prob'ly couldn't find him again!"

Finally she burrowed into a particularly thick growth of bush, spread the oiled cover, carried her pitiful remaining gear into the shelter, and half dragged, half carried the almost comatose Neddy into it.

Somewhere a cow bawled; somewhere a dog barked; somewhere—not unreasonably far away—a milk pail clanged. Wrapping Mama's quilt around them, Holly laid Neddy's hot cheek on her shoulder, rocked him gently, and in a quavering voice comforted him in the only way she knew: "Nonee-no, nonee-no, nonee-no, nonee-no," until she, too, fell asleep.

She awoke to the sound of singing. The morning sun twinkled through the trees, birds twittered nearby, and—carrying sweetly and softly on the fresh air—the faint sound of a simple tune reached into the hiding place.

Rousing, Neddy said, "I'm thirsty, Sissy."

Holly clapped a hand over her brother's mouth and whispered, "Ssshhh—someone is out there."

Finally, loosing her hand, she murmured in Neddy's

ear, "Be quiet—stay here—I'm going to see what—who that is."

Creeping through the bush, Holly peered out toward a meadow and numerous cows grazing peacefully. The tune came again, this time close at hand. Shifting her gaze, Holly looked through the bars of a fence at a small enclosed place—and in the enclosure three small mounds.

With "mounds" Holly was well familiar. These even had a headboard of sorts. Squinting against the sun, she read, "SUFFER THE LITTLE CHILDREN TO COME UNTO ME."

Sitting in the grasses among the small graves, tenderly pulling a weed or two, watering from a can three small rosebushes, her graying head bowed in concentration, her gentle hands working lovingly, a woman sang. Softly, unmistakably, she sang:

Little children, little children . . .
Are the jewels, precious jewels . . .

Almost mesmerized, Holly watched. And surely she made no sound. Perhaps it was Neddy's crawl that gave them away. Perhaps heart called to heart.

When Neddy's small, sunburned face joined Holly's and, crouching, they parted the bushes and looked out— two lonely, lost, homeless, love-hungry children—they saw the woman's face, her motherly face, lift toward them. They saw her eyes fill with comprehension. They saw her lips smile as though with recognition.

Getting to her feet, they watched her take a quick step toward them; they saw her hands reach out toward them. They heard—or would always suppose they had—her joyous but half-whispered words, "Come, little ones, come— unto me."

30

WHEN MATTHEW HUNTER STEPPED OFF THE train, he stepped into the midday hustle and bustle of a thriving little town. Here the old and the new joined hearts in one passionate purpose, and hands in one powerful effort to accomplish it.

Graceful carriages driven by blooded horses jostled worn farm wagons pulled by plodding plow horses; gingham-clad elbows brushed the latest puff-top sleeves; sunbonnets nodded to towering creations of jet and lace and plume; manured boots and lumbermen's packs walked the streets in cadence with satin calf and patent leather.

Raw storefronts bid for business side by side with well-established brick edifices. One of the first things to catch Matthew's attention was a hulking building grandly called an "emporium"; the second was that it was named "Vaughn's Royal Emporium."

Thoughtfully he stepped into the hotel and inquired, "Can you tell me where Vaughn House is?" It was the address to which he had written Hannah when he proposed.

"Yes, of course. Everyone knows Vaughn House. It's that big place on the hill. But if you're looking for Miss Hannah, she's probably at the emporium this time of day."

Matthew's heart sank; his suspicions, it seemed, were about to come true.

Most men might have passed through the store in anything from overalls to a fancy cassimere plaid suit and caused little or no stir. As it was, numerous female eyes lingered appreciatively on the wide shoulders filling out the gray corduroy coat and the long legs in their purposeful stride—lingered and appreciated until the bronzed face turned and the livid scar shone in the semi-gloom of the building. Many a gasp was stifled, and eyes flew wide in dismay.

Pausing before what a more observant customer would have recognized as a display of bleached damask towels, Matthew asked a startled clerk, "Is Miss Vaughn in?"

"No, sir, I don't believe so. But you can inquire at the office—" And a nod in the proper direction took Matthew's firm steps toward a man who, upon seeing the stranger's set face, rose from his desk to ask, "What can I do for you?"

"Miss Vaughn—Hannah—where is she?"

Karl Krueger hesitated. "You are—Matthew?"

"You have the advantage, sir," Matthew's voice was cold.

"Karl Krueger, at your service."

"That remains to be seen, Mr. Krueger. You are—manager of this establishment." Matthew's eyes flicked toward the name and title on the desk. "And the owner, I assume"—his voice had a dangerous edge to it—"is Hannah. Hannah Vaughn. Hannah Vaughn Hunter."

"Sit down, Matthew," Karl Krueger said gently and went to the door and closed it. "I think we need to talk."

"I don't need explanations from Hannah's manager, Mr. Krueger!"

"But perhaps from her friend. Please, Matthew—"

Matthew, perplexed, dismayed, uncertain, sat.

"I don't know what happened between you and Hannah," Karl began, "but you need to know about Hannah's childhood, her miserable relationship with her father—"

"I know about that, Mr. Krueger. Gussie Chapman told me. But that doesn't explain why she would—why she would deceive me in regard to all—this." Matthew's sweeping hand took in the store around them. "Tell me— are there other surprises? Other—resources?"

"Yes," Karl said evenly and thought he detected a groan from the stranger's twisted lips.

"But that changes everything!" Matthew gritted under his breath. "I would never—*never* have considered proposing marriage if I'd known!"

"Are you quite certain of that, Mr. Hunter?" Karl asked quietly.

Matthew raised a surprised face toward the man awaiting what seemed to be a crucial answer. "Why?" he asked. "Why do you ask?"

"Because," Karl said, "the whole plan, from the first, hinged on its importance."

"You see, Matthew, Hannah has been courted for her money, or so she feels, and I think with some reason. Finally, she got so she didn't trust any man's motive, convinced from her father's opinion that no one would want her for any other reason."

Matthew's dark brows drew together in a frown as he tried to assimilate what Karl was saying.

"I know Hannah, Mr. Hunter. And I know she would have counted everything she owned as nothing if she had found what she was looking for in a man. We had hoped," Karl added gently, "you were that man. Are you?"

The room was an island of silence amid the muted activity all around. Matthew, eyes thoughtful, finally rose to his feet, reached across the desk, shook the hand of Karl Krueger, and said, "Now if you'll tell me how I can find her—"

❋   ❋   ❋

Hannah entered the parlor, leaned her trembling body against the door at her back, and looked across the living room at the man standing quietly in front of the massive mirror over the fireplace.

For the longest moment Hannah looked at the intent face, saw too Matthew's image reflected in the mirror at his back, and herself etched against the dark paneling.

Herself—Hannah Vaughn—and she saw again the despised pallor; she saw Hannah's simple dress, the unfortunately tumbled hair. She saw the slender form—taller than it should be, thinner than acceptable. She saw the vulnerable mouth and the haunted eyes.

She saw the figure of the man. She saw it stir, she heard him speak, vibrantly, words fraught with meaning and memory:

"Hello—*wife*."

She saw the transformation as it dawned in the pale mirrored face; she saw the mouth open in a choked cry of pure joy; she saw the body take its first step from the door that had supported it, saw it run, saw its arms go out to meet the hands stretched toward it, saw it wrapped in the arms waiting for it.

Saw finally, before her eyes closed in sheer bliss, the dark head of the man as it bent toward the glowing face lifted to it.

What followed—the whispered sweet nothings that said so much, the first endearments that would last a lifetime, and yes, a few tears—was a sight shared only with the "looking glass" as it faithfully reproduced scenes never enacted before it previously and heard words never before uttered in its presence. In that moment its power to belittle and intimidate—if indeed it ever had such power—was shattered forever.

When finally sensible conversation was possible, Matthew freed himself enough to draw a letter from his pocket.

"I think you need to see this, my little love—my lovely little love—" for which superior vocalization he received a rapturous kiss—several of them.

"Dear Mr. Ketcham," Hannah read. "It's my sorry conclusion that the mare you sold me was misrepresented . . . a disappointment, I must say . . . older than you indicated . . . a good worker, no doubt, but nothing to look at . . . a bad bargain . . ."

"Oh!" Hannah struggled to express the mix of emotions that flooded her already-swimming head and soaring heart, and ended by shedding a few more tears—which, of course, must needs be kissed away.

When a semblance of rationality had once again been established, Matthew's eyes lit with purpose. "Let's go home," he urged. "And let's go right away. Can you be ready in, say, two hours?"

"I never unpacked—I'm ready," Hannah confessed and received a kiss for her cleverness. "That is," she said thoughtfully, "except to add one item."

The looking glass, left behind in a dim house that would eventually brighten and echo with the voices of boys and girls under the tender care of Tilda and Malachi in Delbert Bly's "Home for Indigent Children," was left to wonder about what turned out to be, after all, just a small, three-inch, three-cent biscuit cutter.

Experience the
Other Wildrose Adventures . . .

The Shining Light

The promise of land and a new life in the West was a shining light that beckoned. Together, Worth and Abbie could carve out a new existence in the Saskatchewan Territory—but can Abbie hold on to the dream alone.

Bitter Thistle, Sweet Rose

After being deeply hurt already, how could Linn be so naive—and wrong—to fall in love again? This is a compelling story of romance and faith, intertwining Linn's journey with that of other unforgettable characters from Wildrose.

A Time to Dream

Young and optimistic, Rob and Cassie Quinn joined the bands of immigrants converging on the vast Northwest Territories. But Cassie was alone now, except for the child—hers and Rob's—that struggled within her body. What dreams are left for Cassie and her unborn baby?

The Shining Light	BF083-411-514X	**$9.99**
Bitter Thistle, Sweet Rose	BF083-411-528X	**$9.99**
A Time to Dream	BF083-411-5725	**$9.99**

Purchase from your favorite bookstore
or order toll-free from:
BEACON HILL PRESS OF KANSAS CITY
1-800-877-0700